Arthur Ness
and the
Secret of Waterwhistle

Part 1

wilf morgan

BRING A WORLD OF ADVENTURE TO YOUR SCHOOL!

Want to do something cool for your school? Show this book to your teacher, reading co-ordinator, librarian... heck, just barge right into the Headteacher's office! Then say these words;

"Hi! (Sorry for knocking over your goldfish). If you send an email to **free-books@88tales.com**, you'll get a free 88Tales Press book for the school! One per school, Terms and Conditions on the **88tales.com** website. Okay, I'll go and get a mop."

Then sit back and await hero status. Easy!

88TALES PRESS
Southwell, Nottinghamshire,
NG25 0DF
www.88tales.com

First published in Great Britain
in 2017 by 88Tales Alpha
an imprint of 88Tales Press

First Edition

A catalogue record for this book is
available from the British Library

ISBN 978 1 9997590 3 2

www.88tales.com

www.arilon-chronicles.com

Thanks to Tia, Jake and Joe for pestering
me until I wrote this book!

(Now, go and tidy your rooms.)

Acknowledgements

Thanks to all the kids (even the adult-sized ones..!) who read early versions of this book and gave me invaluable feedback. I literally couldn't have done it without you.

Akeira, Andrea, Anna, Chloe, Debbie, Fola, Gareth, Jacob D, Jakey, Jane, Jocelyn, Joe II, Joseph M, Josh, Kaleb, Lewis, Lionel, Mark, Murray, Sam, Samuel D, Tia, Usman

Special thanks as well to the Bookcase in Lowdham, Nottinghamshire for all the support and advice and also to the staff and pupils at Sneinton C of E Primary School for all the priceless input!

Over 2000 years ago, in Rome, a man called Virgil said

'Fortune favours the bold'

Or to put it another way;

'Be brave! You never know - you might just get lucky and win...'

PROLOGUE

Arthur Ness ran.

He ran so fast that his chest was bursting, his head was pounding and his legs were burning up from the inside. *You'd best stop running right now,* his legs threatened him. *Or we'll never work for you again!*

But Arthur Ness did not stop running. One of the witch's spells blasted right past his head. Its bright, white light slammed into a nearby wall and the explosion blasted stone and mortar in all directions.

Arthur Ness ran faster.

Somewhat unnecessarily, the talking cat next to him shouted, "Keep running, Arthur!"

There were times that Arthur Ness needed advice – like what to do about the boys at school that bullied him. Or whether it was okay to feel bad that his father was off fighting Hitler in the war (when he knew he was supposed to feel proud). Or how to handle being scared of everything all the time. Yes, all those things Arthur gladly admitted that he could do with some advice on.

Being chased by an evil witch and several huge, snarling bull-creatures that ran on their hind legs and brandished giant swords and axes..? No, he didn't need advice on that. He knew *just* what to do.

"Arthur Ness!" screeched the witch. "You cannot escape! There is nowhere to run to!"

"Don't listen to her, Arthur," the cat called. "One thing I've learned in all my lives is that there's *always* somewhere to run to! Just keep going!"

Easy for you to say, thought Arthur, *you've got four legs!*

Nevertheless, having the cat with him, even though they were running for their lives, somehow made Arthur feel better.

A little.

"This way!" the cat shouted impossibly loudly while darting left through a stone doorway. "We're seconds away from a grand escape!" Arthur huffed and puffed and put his head down and sprinted after him. The doorway was ancient and medieval-looking just like the rest of the castle and it was identical to a hundred other doorways they'd passed. Arthur didn't have the spare energy to wonder just how the cat knew his way around this place or where they were going. But even though he'd only known the creature for a short time and even though this was, admittedly, the first talking cat he'd ever met and even though he'd never really liked cats in the first place... Arthur trusted him. So he followed the cat through the doorway.

It led outside.

To a cliff.

Which meant that they were-

"-trapped..!" Arthur gasped in-between deep gulps of breath. "I thought you said this way was a grand escape?"

"Jumping off a cliff isn't a grand escape where you're from?" The cat shook his head. "You're a picky one, Arthur Ness."

Instead of safety, the cat had led them to a dead end. Arthur looked around quickly as his rasping, heaving lungs fought to suck air back into his body. But while his breathing slowed, Arthur's brain began race as he noticed the strangeness of his new surroundings.

They were outside the castle now and Arthur saw how big the place really was. Dozens of grey, forbidding battlements and towers clawed their way up to the sky. A perfectly black sky with no stars. Just a big, round, white moon.

And yet...

The moon's harsh, white light burned at Arthur's eyes and he had to quickly look away. There was only one thing that burned so brightly you couldn't look directly at it, Arthur knew. That was no moon. That was a sun.

A sun at night.

Arthur looked down and tried to blink away the green and yellow spots the ball of white flame had sent dancing across his vision. As his sight cleared, he saw that the cliff they were standing on stretched away down to... well, nothing. No ground, no sea. Just more blackness, the same as the sky. Perhaps it was so dark, the bottom was just hidden, Arthur thought. But no, the cliff face didn't fade away into darkness. It just... stopped. Right where the darkness began. It was as if the black, empty sky was wrapped all the way around them – above and below.

The final thing Arthur noticed was a cable attached to the ground, right next to where he and the cat were standing. It was a massive thing – wider and thicker than Arthur's body – and it stretched up and away into the black sky. Unlike the cliff, the cable did fade away into the darkness and Arthur could tell it went out a long way, further than he could see. But what on Earth was it attached to? What was sitting out there, out of sight, holding on to this thing?

Given all this strangeness, Arthur was more than a little unsettled that the cat was so unshakably calm. Especially as the witch was now emerging from the doorway behind them, her massive, armed Yarnbulls flanking her, left and right.

"Ah, Eris," said the cat, "so glad you could keep up. I thought we might have lost you what with all the twisting and turning and... you know... trying to lose you."

Lady Eris raised a hand toward them, energy sparking dangerously between her fingers.

"So, Arthur Ness..." she sneered, her eyes dark, her breath not at all heavy or rasping like his, "...and you, my feline tormentor... your running is finally at an end."

That's when the huge, stretched-out cable began to shake.

And shake.

And shake.

And the cat smiled.

ARTHUR NESS
AND THE
SECRET OF WATERWHISTLE

PART I

THREAD ONE

THE CAT IN THE CARPET

THE BIG HOUSE
AT THE END OF THE VILLAGE

Arthur Ness was scared. Of everything.

It was almost Christmas of 1940 and Arthur was a long way from home. Enemy planes were flying over London every night and bombing everything, including his own neighbourhood. His mother was still there, alone. His father, a pilot in the RAF, was somewhere in the skies above, facing constant death, battling the enemy. So, perhaps it could be argued that Arthur had many good reasons to be scared of everything.

Unfortunately, Arthur's fear had been around a lot longer than the war. It had been with him for his entire life. He'd been scared of his first teddy bear (and his second... and his third). He'd been scared of his neighbour because she was too old. He'd been scared of going under his bed. He'd been scared of climbing trees. Of going swimming. Of animals. Of the strange way his cousin's dolls looked at him.

Now, right now, Arthur was standing on the doorstep of a big house. It was nighttime and it was raining. He was in a village he'd never heard of, in a part of the country that was miles away from his home. He was standing on that doorstep getting wetter and wetter and colder and colder.

And he was too scared to knock.

"You have to be brave," his mum said as they

stood on the platform in the train station. There were other children, other parents all around. The platform was packed with them. Some he recognised from school, most not. Arthur didn't look at his mother. If he didn't look at her, the conversation couldn't finish. If the conversation didn't finish, she couldn't put him on the train. If he didn't get put on the train, he wouldn't get sent away like all these other children.

But his mum gently took hold of Arthur's chin and turned his face toward hers. And she smiled at him.

"Be brave, okay?" she said. "For me."

And Arthur nodded.

And then the conversation did finish. And he did get put on the train. And he did get sent away with all the other children. And even though he knew it was making him safe from the bombs, Arthur had never felt so alone. Or afraid.

Arthur sneezed.

The rain was beginning to soak through his clothes. His cap, his coat, his shorts – even his socks inside his shoes. All beginning to get squelchy and horrible and cold. His little, battered suitcase was looking exceedingly soggy. And the label that was hanging from the top button of his coat that made him look like a bedraggled, misplaced parcel that nobody wanted. The label that read:

Arthur Ness to :
Lord and Lady Roberts
No.1 Church Lane

Even that was getting hard to read – all the inky words now running into each other in a black, blobby mess.

Blinking against the rain, Arthur forced himself to look up at the house. It was huge and dark with horrid sharp edges and massive windows that looked like evil eyes staring out over the countryside. It even had a small turret at the top, near the roof. Arthur shivered – and not just from the cold.

What kind of a person could possibly live here?

*The kind of person who will be very angry with you
for waking them up at this hour of the night.*

That was the voice. Arthur's voice. Not the one he talked with. It was the one he *thought* with. The one that sat inside his brain and constantly reminded him how scared he was. Arthur never argued with it. It was always right.

But scared or not, Arthur knew this couldn't go on. If he didn't go inside, he would freeze to death. And he didn't *like* freezing to death, not especially.

He took a deep breath and raised his hand toward the wooden door – but before he could knock…

CLANK! CLUNK!

Arthur nearly jumped out of his skin as the deafening noise burst from behind the door. The noise of someone pulling open large, old, heavy locks. Then the door scraped slowly open. And there, emerging from the darkness inside the house into the half-light of the rainy night was the tallest woman Arthur had ever seen.

"Arthur Ness," she said. "You're late."

LADY ERIS

As soon as she said his name, something dark and heavy seemed to land on Arthur's shoulders. His knees went weak and his head felt fuzzy.

"I'm sorry," Arthur muttered, dredging his voice up from the murky depths of his fear. "There was no-one to meet me at the train station in Nottingham. This man with a lorry-full of sheep gave me a lift to Lowdham, but then I had to walk the rest of the -"

"In," she said.

So, in Arthur went. The door slammed shut behind him.

Even though it was nighttime, it was somehow darker inside the house than it was outside. A couple of murky-looking lamps struggled to illuminate a long, high hallway. It was nothing like the houses in London. Not like the ones he'd ever been in, anyway. It was big and quiet and reminded Arthur of being in a church. But not the friendly kind where he went with his parents every Sunday. Here, there were no welcoming smiles or biscuits. Just a wide, sweeping darkness.

Arthur's teeth chattered uncontrollably as he stared up at the dark, towering figure that was glaring down at him.

"Get used to the cold. You are forbidden to put on any heating in this house," the tall woman said to Arthur in a hard, impassable voice. "You will sleep tonight. Tomorrow you will begin work. Every day, you will clean, tidy, cook and wash. You will not speak to me unless it is absolutely necessary. You will stay out of my room. You will stay out of the drawing room. All other rooms are your responsibility to clean. Am I making myself perfectly clear, Arthur Ness?"

"Yes, Lady Roberts," said Arthur. "But, I…"

"I am not Lady Roberts," she said, annoyance crawling all over her voice. "You will call me Lady Eris."

"I'm sorry, Lady Eris," said Arthur, lowering his eyes to the floor, confused and embarrassed.

"Do you have any questions?" she asked. Arthur forced himself to look up at her. She was really very pretty, he thought, but in a dangerous, cruel kind of way. She reminded him of the creatures he'd read about in ancient Greek mythology – Sirens. Beautiful creatures on the outside but nasty and evil within. Her strong jawline and long, black hair framed dark eyes which pinned Arthur, petrified, to the spot. She had on a long, midnight-black dress that seemed to suck in the light around it. It was so long, in fact, that her feet were completely hidden from view. Arthur wondered if she even *had* feet.

"Let us be perfectly clear, Arthur Ness," she said, looking down her nose at the boy. "I do not want you here. It was the previous owners of this house, Lord and Lady Roberts, who volunteered to take in evacuee children from your war. Despite my objections, I was unable to have you sent elsewhere when I… took over."

Arthur nodded, his gaze returning to his feet. *Your* war? What an odd thing to say. Surely, it was everybody's war. Arthur found himself wishing that those Roberts people were here now. They, at least, sounded kind.

Arthur shuffled from foot to foot, unable to settle or calm himself down. Then, quite suddenly, a chill like a hundred daggers swept right through his body. Incredibly, he felt as though Lady Eris was looking *into* him. Into his brain, into his mind. It felt for all the world as though she were spreading his thoughts out like a newspaper on a table and flicking through the pages at her leisure. And then, just like that, the feeling passed and Arthur felt alone in his head once more.

He looked up at her to see a horrid, satisfied grin across Lady Eris' face and he knew just what she was thinking. He knew because he was thinking it too:

You're scared of her, scaredy-cat. Really, really scared. So scared,
you'll do exactly as she says. You won't cause her any trouble.
And she knows it.

Lady Eris unfolded a long arm and pointed a slender finger up the stairs.

"Your room is the first on the left," she said. "Mine is across the way, up in the tower. Never go there."

Arthur looked up towards where she was pointing. When he turned to look back at her, he was startled to find her face just inches away from his.

"*Never,*" she repeated, "go there."

Arthur nodded, mute.

Suddenly, he noticed her hair. Up close like this, it almost looked like lots and lots of pieces of straight, black...

...string?

Lady Eris returned to her full height.

"Go. Unpack. Sleep," she said. "Tomorrow, you begin."

Without waiting for another word from her young houseguest, the scariest woman Arthur had ever met turned and went into the drawing room – one of the two rooms he was already banned from.

As the door to the room swung slowly open, Arthur caught a glimpse of something inside – the biggest, most elaborate tapestry he had ever seen. Okay, he had to admit he hadn't seen many tapestries. But this one was absolutely huge. A great piece of material, like a wall-mounted rug. It stretched from floor to ceiling and was made entirely from multi-coloured cotton threads, woven in and out to make a huge picture.

Actually, Arthur noticed, it was lots of little pictures, all connected to each other from one end of the weaving to the other. But the pictures were too small for Arthur to make out at this range. All except one.

The picture of a small, black cat.

Arthur wasn't sure why that one caught his eye. Maybe because it looked kind of different from the other images. A different style. The cat was looking off to one side. Very enigmatic, Arthur thought. Impressive. Mysterious.

A drop of rainwater plopped off the end of his cap and landed on his nose, making Arthur sneeze.

When he looked back up at the cat again, Arthur was somewhat startled to see that the cat was looking back at him.

And - **click** - the door closed, leaving Arthur standing in almost total darkness.

With a sigh and a shake of his head, the young Londoner picked up his heavy bag and suitcase. He was exhausted. Scared. Not thinking straight. Clearly, he'd looked at a different picture the second time. Clearly, it hadn't *actually* moved. Clearly, he needed sleep.

And so Arthur trudged up the stairs, his case banging on each step as he went.

OUT OF THE TAPESTRY
(from the chaotic thoughts of the Cat)

The ship was on fire.

If I had to make a list of sentences I want to say while aboard a ship, they would include 'I'm going to take a long nap', 'Yes, madam, you're right, I *am* handsome' and my all-time favourite, 'I see that everything on the menu is made of fish.'

'The ship's on fire' wouldn't even make the top one hundred. When I got aboard this morning, the Captain had assured me his vessel was sturdy and strong and reliable and absolutely *not* going to be on fire by late afternoon. Still, I suppose it wasn't entirely his fault. I'd say the fault lay more in the hands of the Royal Battle Ships that were attacking us.

Now, as bad as things were – and, make no mistake, being under attack from the Queen's Royal Vanguard is very bad indeed – things could actually have been worse.

'You were on board a ship that was on fire!' I hear you cry. 'How could things have been worse?!'

Well, mainly because nobody knew I was here. I mean, yes the Captain and his crew. But they just thought I was a normal talking cat. They thought the same thing everyone thinks when they see me. What a nice cat. What a small cat. What a harmless cat.

In reality, I'm none of those things.

So, since the Captain and the crew thought I was just a regular (if dashingly handsome) cat and since the Queen's soldiers – like the Queen herself – thought I was already dead (more on that later) then that meant they hadn't attacked the ship because they were looking for me.

Like I said, that was a good thing. It meant my mission could go ahead. Well, once I'd dealt with the whole 'trying not to be on fire' thing.

'And how did you do that?' I hear you cry.

Well, have no fear. I may be a small, black cat (or I may not) but I'm perfectly capable of taking care of myself. Little cat. Flaming ship careening toward the docks at full speed. No problem.

I've been in plenty of scrapes in my time – most of them courtesy of the Queen. I've spent more years than I care to remember fighting her. Yes, many years and four lives. Fighting either her or one of her Noir Ladies.

In fact, when it comes to the Noir Ladies, I've got a one hundred percent record. I've seen off each and every one of them. Lady Aerie. Lady Kray. Lady Taranteen. Several others. All defeated. And each time, the Queen doesn't get the hint. She just goes ahead and brings out a new model. The latest one, though… ooh, she's a toughie.

Lady Eris.

By far, the meanest, coldest and most dangerous of all the Queen's Noir Ladies. We've been battling for some months now. Even in that short space of time, though, we've gotten to know each other quite well, I'd say. Best of friends. Do anything for each other.

By 'best of friends', of course, I mean, 'worst of enemies'. And by 'do anything for each other' I mean 'kill each other on sight'.

In fact, the last time we met (a couple of weeks ago on board a runaway train heading into the heart of an active volcano, very exciting) she dealt me what baddies like to call a 'killer blow'. She thought she'd finally defeated me once and for all. Thought I was on my last life.

She'd miscounted.

However, even though I escaped (fantastic stunt, it was, remind me to tell you how I did it), I have to admit that none of the Queen's other Noir Ladies have ever come as close to defeating me as Lady Eris. And under her stewardship, the Queen's schemes have actually started to get quite... well... *lethal.*

Up until now, my battles with the Queen were lots of fun. She'd come up with some villainous scheme and I'd stop her. She'd rant and rave for a bit. Then she'd come up with another villainous scheme and the whole shindig would start all over again.

Except now, with Lady Eris at the helm, the Queen's villainous doings are actually starting to work. I can't defeat her quite so easily.

Occasionally, I can't defeat her at all.

More and more of my allies are getting captured, killed or Bound. More and more of hers are running wild. She's always had her agents – you know, the soldiers, the Yarnbulls, the Sharp-Eyes (oh, and the Rainhand – if you can count that terrible, terrible creature as truly *hers*...). But now, everything feels like it's almost in the palm of her hand. The sun, the islands and all the NothingSpace in between. (By the way, I'm glad you're from Arilon – if you were some random human, you wouldn't have a clue what I'm going on about).

Anyway, I keep getting sidetracked.

Me. Flaming ship. Speeding towards the docks on Noir Island. Location of Noir Castle. Home of Lady Eris of the Noir Ladies (okay, I'm sure you'd figured all that out).

Now, let me assure you, once again, that I'm really very amazing and extremely talented when it comes to getting out of tight scrapes.

'But how?!' I hear you cry. (You really ought to stop with all the crying. It's bound to get us discovered).

You see, I had a plan. Well, it wasn't really a plan – I just ran as fast as I could and hoped no-one saw me. I hate plans. Plans are boring. Knowing what's going to happen in advance? Where's the fun in that?

So, anyway, I had the utmost confidence in my abilities and I *did* manage to get off the blazing ship before it crashed into the island. And I *did* manage to do it without being seen. And I *did* manage to evade all the soldiers and Yarnbulls roaming the castle as I made my way to the Main Hall.

And I did manage to get into the tapestry and make my way over to the Human World. All the way to Waterwhistle.

And guess what I saw as I arrived in the drawing room in the house in the village in the Human World? Guess what I saw standing there, shivering and dripping wet?

I saw a young, frightened human boy.

And I thought '*brilliant*'.

Because I knew I'd just found the best weapon against the Queen I could ever have hoped to find.

THE SILENCE OF WATERWHISTLE

One day into his stay, Arthur had decided he hated the countryside. After another four days, he'd revised his opinion.

He *really* hated the countryside.

Arthur had muddled his way through most of his first week in Waterwhistle and he was really beginning to miss the city. Right now, as he trudged through the village, pushing a wheelbarrow over the rough gravel of the village square, Arthur felt the nasty, oppressive nature of the countryside.

First of all – and most scary – were the hills. They were just…*there*. Right there, all around. Looking at him.

There was nothing like them in London. And if there were any hills, they were sensibly covered up with lots and lots of buildings. Here, the hills were left standing bare and proud. And the open spaces – wow, the open spaces just went on and on and on for miles. It was most unnatural.

And as if that wasn't enough, there was also the village itself. The streets were tiny, the buildings were small and most unnerving of all, there were animals wandering around. And not just dogs and cats (they had those in London, he could handle those). It was the *big* animals. The geese. The sheep.

The cows.

Arthur didn't trust the cows. They constantly looked as though they were whispering about him. He kept his distance from the cows.

As strange and disorienting as all this was, though, none of it compared to the worst thing about Waterwhistle. Because the worst thing…

…was the silence.

Arthur had always thought that people in villages were meant to be friendly. Full of community spirit and 'how do you do's and forever lending each other cups of sugar.

Well, not *these* people.

On the very first day, Lady Eris had sent him into town with a wheelbarrow to fetch some compost from the village grocer. And right from that very first day, the silence had been deafening. At first, Arthur had wondered if he'd been imagining it. Was he just used to London noise? People shouting at each other all day (and most of the night)? But no, surely something was definitely wrong.

"How much for six apples?" someone would ask.

"Six pence," the shopkeeper would reply.

This constituted the longest conversation Arthur had yet overheard. But when money and apples changed hands and then shopkeeper and customer went their separate ways without even a 'Thank you, bye!', Arthur knew something strange was going on.

Even the children didn't make any noise. He'd seen some on his first day. They were in the park. Some were sat on swings, some on the roundabout. A couple on a see-saw. And they were swinging and see-sawing and roundabouting. But not talking. It was like their bodies were there, but their minds were mostly somewhere else.

Arthur had hurried on by.

So, all in all, Arthur wasn't a great fan of the countryside. When faced with all that, being told to scrub floors and polish staircases all day didn't seem so bad. At least he was inside.

Unfortunately, though, Lady Eris had given him another job to do. One that needed compost. And lots of it. So here he was, collecting what felt like his hundredth bag.

"Good morning, Mr. Smith!" Arthur chirped his greeting as he pushed his empty wheelbarrow in through the doorway of the grocer's. As always, the place was full of people buying fresh fruit and veg in almost total silence.

Arthur said, "I'm here for Lady Eris' compost, as usual." He always tried to be polite, even though the response was always exactly the same.

Mr. Smith was a tall, broad man with a receding hairline, a firm jaw and no hint of anything remotely resembling a smile. He pressed something on the till and it **ping**ed open. He held out his hand. Arthur dropped the coins into it. Mr. Smith put the coins in the till. He closed it. Then, he turned and disappeared out to the back of the shop.

All without a word.

Arthur shrugged as his eyes caught the front page of the newspaper someone had left on the counter-top. *More Bombings in London* read the headline. Arthur began to crane his head around to see if he could see any-

SNORT!

Arthur's head shot up - what on earth was *that*? A horse, it sounded like. Really close... like, right behind his head! But – he span round – there was nothing there... No horse. And, strangely, even though it had been so loud, no reaction from any of the other shoppers.

"Did…" he stammered to a woman next to him examining some potatoes, "…did you hear that?"

The woman turned and looked at him, quizzically. Her eyes looked Arthur up and down, probably trying to figure out if he was a little bit crazy. Eventually, she shook her head.

"Didn't hear nuthin'."

And she turned back to her potatoes.

A sudden **THUMP** jerked Arthur's head round once again – but it was just Mr Smith. He'd returned with the compost and had dumped the sack into Arthur's wheelbarrow.

"Oh, er…" Arthur gathered his composure again, "…thanks, Mr. Smith."

But Mr. Smith wasn't taking any notice. He'd gone back to staring out of the window.

Grunting, Arthur lifted the handles of his wheelbarrow and left the shop with its strange customers and even stranger sounds.

That's when he heard *another* sound.

Thunk.

Thunk.

Thunk.

This one made Arthur smile, though, because he knew exactly what it was.

Someone was bouncing a football!

THINGS YOU CAN'T SEE

At last! Someone normal!

"Hey!" Arthur called out, plonking his heavy wheelbarrow down on the cobbled street. "Over here! Give us a kick!"

The boy looked up from his one-child game of football. Immediately, a look of fear crossed the boy's face. Arthur had to admit, that hadn't been the expression he was particularly expecting.

The boy looked Arthur up and down, trying to figure the stranger out. Then...

...he rolled the ball over.

Grinning, Arthur flicked the ball up and did a series of keepy-uppies with his knees, feet and (to the boy's amazement) his head. Arthur finished off the show by chesting the ball down, letting it drop to the ground and trapping it under his foot.

"Wow!" the boy uttered his first words, an awestruck grin plastered across his face. "That were brilliant!"

Arthur shrugged, modestly, "Something I saw Ted Drake do when my dad took me to see the Arsenal last year."

For the first time since he'd arrived in Waterwhistle, Arthur felt something other than abject fear. He'd finally met someone who seemed kind of normal. He rolled the ball back to the boy who picked it up, staring at it like it had just been dropped from outer space.

"What's your name?" Arthur asked.

"Sam," said the boy as the smile finally melted off his face. "You're Arthur Ness, aren't you? You live up in the big house. With *her*."

Obviously, the locals felt the same way about Lady Eris as Arthur did. He nodded.

"Yes. She's keeping me busy, that's for sure. Every day, I have to get compost and spread it all over the garden. And she gives me these weird seeds. They're all nobbly and spiky. Horrible things. Never seen anything like them. I don't know what they're meant to grow into…except…"

Sam had a somewhat wary look on his face as Arthur talked but he didn't interrupt. So Arthur – not knowing what else to talk about – decided he might as well press on.

"…well, sometimes, when I go into the garden, there are big holes there. I mean, massive. Almost big enough for me to fit into. Like something's been pulled out in the night. But…well, it can't be, can it? Because there's nothing growing there during the day."

Sam stood there, turning the football over and over in his hands as he watched Arthur, his earlier grin of admiration long gone. The awkward silence made Arthur look down at his feet and start tapping a stone with the toe of his shoe.

"Everyone's afraid, y'know," Sam suddenly said. Arthur looked up, intrigued.

"Afraid? Afraid of what?"

"Not of 'what'…" said Sam, "…of '*who*'."

"Alright, then, of *who*?"

The ball suddenly stopped dead still in Sam's hands.

"Lady Eris."

SNORT!

Arthur snapped his head up – that noise, again! It had to be a horse, it was so clear this time, so loud!

"Did you hear that?" Arthur said. When he looked back at Sam, he expected to see the same look of bewilderment that the grown-ups in the grocer's had had. But, Sam didn't look bewildered. He looked scared.

"I didn't hear nothin'," he said, evenly. And Arthur could tell right away. Sam was lying.

A horrible feeling was beginning to build in Arthur's stomach but he didn't know exactly why. Something told him not to ask Sam why he was pretending he couldn't hear the noises.

"So…you were saying," Arthur said, "about Lady Eris..? That everyone's scared of her?"

"Well, not *exactly* everyone," said the boy, a new note of pride in his voice. "My sister weren't."

Arthur was immediately interested. Brave people always intrigued him.

"And where is she?" he asked. "Your sister?"

The boy held his ball in one hand and pointed gingerly over toward the village square. "She were standing there. Shoutin'. Tellin' people how Lady Eris were doin' somethin' to 'em. How she were makin' the town all…silent."

Aha, thought Arthur, so the silence *wasn't* normal.

"And were people listening?" Arthur asked.

"Oh, yeah." The boy nodded. "People were startin' to gather. There were a bit of a crowd. As Teresa – that's me sister's name – as Teresa talked, you could see some people noddin' and agreein' with her."

"So, what happened?"

"She vanished."

Arthur was taken aback. "What do you mean, vanished?"

"One second she were there," said Sam, quietly, "the next second, she weren't. It were like she were taken. Taken by things you couldn't see."

Arthur shivered. He didn't like the sound of this.

SCRAPE

Arthur jerked his head again. What was that sound? Like hooves on cobblestones. Perhaps it-

GRUNT

It was just village noises, he thought. It had to be. In fact, at the far end of the street, there was a farmer with a horse and trap cart. He was lifting heavy sacks onto the back of it. It must have been him grunting and his horse's hooves scraping.

Except, it had sounded so *close*...

"What did the people say?" Arthur asked, ignoring the noise once again. "When your sister vanished? What did they do?"

"Nothin'." Sam shrugged. "They just walked away. No-one even talks about it. Like they can't remember it ever happenin'."

Sam was talking nonsense, Arthur decided. He had to be. People forgetting something the instant after they watched it happen? This all sounded so unlikely, so pretend, so crazy.

And yet, there were the noises...

"But *you* remember," said Arthur. "Didn't you see what took her?"

Sam was silent for a long time. Then he finally looked Arthur in the eye and whispered. "Sometimes, it's best not

to notice dangerous things. If you can't see them, they can't hurt you."

Arthur felt cold all over. Then...

SNORT!

... a blast of warm air rushed down his back. He span round. That one was right behind him!

"Arthur," Sam's tone was suddenly desperate and urgent, his voice still a whisper and it made Arthur turn to face him again. "I think it were Lady Eris what took Teresa. You're livin' up there. Can you look? Can you look for her? She must be up there somewhere!"

"But..." Arthur didn't possess the words to describe to Sam how scared he was of Lady Eris, "...she's very strict. She tells me what to do and where to go and..."

"*Please*," Sam was standing right in front of Arthur, now, his voice even more desperate. "She's me *sister*..."

Arthur's mind was swimming. He didn't see how he could possibly help Sam. But given that this was the first person to speak to him in a friendly way, he didn't see how he could possibly *not*.

He opened his mouth to answer when Sam's eyes suddenly widened in horror. He was looking directly above and behind Arthur. Shot through with fear, Arthur span round. What was it? What was there?!

Nothing.

Nothing was there.

His heart thumping, he turned back to Sam but the boy had already begun walking off. He wasn't bouncing the ball now. He was acting like everyone else. Silent. Scared.

Suddenly, Arthur decided his nerves had taken enough. He jogged back over to his wheelbarrow, hefted the handles up and made his way as quickly as he could back through the village. He had to get this wet, stinky stuff back to the big house. Then he had to spread it all over the garden before he got in trouble. Time to put this nonsense out of his mind. Because, it *was* nonsense, wasn't it?

He took one last glance over his shoulder. He looked at the spot where he thought he'd heard strange noises and felt strange things.

But it was just empty space.

What was it Sam had said?

Sometimes, it's best not to notice dangerous things.

LADY ERIS' ROOM

"Put your back into it, Arthur Ness!" Lady Eris scolded the young boy, her voice devoid of any mercy. "I want that floor scrubbed and scrubbed and scrubbed again."

Not even daring to pause to catch his breath, Arthur, down on his knees, dunked the scrubbing brush into the bucket of dirty water. He sloshed it around for a second before putting it back on the hard, wooden floor and carried on scrubbing.

He'd been at this for almost an hour. Not the rest of the floors in the house, just this one area. The upstairs landing that linked Lady Eris' room and his. He had started outside his own room, worked his way along the corridor, up the four or five steps to the higher part of the landing and was now finally outside the turret on the corner of the house. Lady Eris' room.

Arthur's knees scraped against the rough, wooden floorboards. His back was aching, his shoulders and arms were burning and his hands and fingers were red raw from pushing this blummin' brush back and forth, trying to clean wooden panels that – to Arthur, anyway – really didn't seem that dirty.

Arthur had been in this house for a couple of weeks now and in all that time, he barely saw Lady Eris anywhere other than her room and the drawing room where the giant tapestry was. She barely spent any time in any other part of the house. And yet, Arthur had to spend all his time keeping it all clean. And what for? She didn't care about how clean the place was, that much was obvious.

In fact, Arthur had the distinct impression that she was simply keeping him busy and out of the way while she did...

...what?

Could Sam have been telling the truth? Could Lady Eris be up to something in this place? And if she was, Arthur thought, shouldn't he do something about it...?

Like what? What could you do about it, scaredy-cat? Absolutely nothing. Because you're unimportant.

Arthur knew the voice was right, so he kept on scrubbing.

"And don't even think about eating dinner until this entire floor is spotless, Arthur Ness," she said.

"No, ma'am."

"And after you've eaten, don't you dare go to bed until you've cleaned the downstairs hallway again."

"No, ma'am."

And with that, Lady Eris turned and went into her room, her unseen feet banging out a firm **click clunk click clunk** with every step. Not daring to look up or stop scrubbing for even a second, Arthur waited for the sound of Lady Eris' bedroom door closing. At least then he could rest for a second. He waited and waited. But the sound never came. He glanced up.

Lady Eris had left her door ever so slightly ajar.

From his position, Arthur could see right into her room for the first time. Nervously, he craned his neck forward a little and stole a peek further into the room. It didn't look anything special. But he saw something much more interesting than what kind of wardrobe she had.

Lady Eris was dancing.

Arthur couldn't believe his eyes. This horrid, stern woman was actually, actually dancing! A weird dance it was, too. All in the arms. It was like she was playing some kind of huge, invisible harp. He could almost see her plucking the strings this way and that, first on one side of the room and then the other, back and forth.

Suddenly, a brief glimmer of light caught Arthur's eye and he noticed something else in the room – a safe. It was in the far wall, beyond Lady Eris. And it was slightly open. Even from where he was, Arthur could see that there was only one thing inside the safe. A small, shiny hand mirror.

Arthur started to wonder what was so special about a mirror that it would be the only thing to be put into the safe when he suddenly noticed two things –

One) at some point over the last few seconds, he'd stopped scrubbing...

...and Two) Lady Eris was standing still as a statue.

Staring right at him.

Arthur's heart leapt in his chest in embarrassment and he quickly shifted his eyes back down to the floor and went back to scrubbing twice as hard as before. He didn't dare look up and all he heard was the **click clunk** of Lady Eris walking towards him and a **BANG** as the door was slammed shut, leaving him alone on the landing.

THE CAT

The rest of Arthur's day was like all the other days in the big house and it went like this;

CLEAN
SCRUB
WASH
SPREAD COMPOST
CLEAN
SCRUB
SCRUB
SCRUB
SPREAD COMPOST
WASH
CLEAN
WASH
SCRUB
SPREAD COMPOST

And it ended with

CLIMB THE STAIRS
CHANGE INTO PYJAMAS
COLLAPSE INTO BED

Arthur had done CLIMB THE STAIRS by forcing his tired, aching arms and legs up the staircase one agonising step at a time. Exhausted, he then slowly did CHANGE INTO PYJAMAS (it made him sad that his pyjamas now no longer smelled of home – they just smelled of here). Finally, he started COLLAPSE INTO BED by turning toward his bed and –

"Woah!" Arthur jumped in fright and almost fell backwards when he saw what was on his bed.

A cat.

"Where did *you* come from?!" Arthur tried to calm his suddenly thumping heart. "I've never seen you before. How did you get in here?"

The cat was small and black and radiated an air of regal calm. It sat on Arthur's pillow like it was a throne. No longer would the pillow be used for anything as mundane as resting Arthur's head on – it had been upgraded to something far more important, now.

It blinked at him.

Surprising himself, Arthur laughed.

"Listen to me, I'm going crazy." He allowed himself a tiny smile, his eyes still looking at the feline. "I'm talking to a cat!"

"Yes," said the cat. "Imagine if I talked back."

"Aaaahh!"

This time Arthur *did* fall over. Right over. Onto his backside, knocking his empty suitcase and sending it skidding across the floor. His eyes and mouth were wide open and he pointed a shaking finger at the small, black creature.

"You…you…" Arthur stammered, "you…you…"

"Me, me, me?" said the cat. "Ah, fantastic! You're a clever one. You just worked out my favourite topic of conversation. Let's talk about *me!*"

"You can… you can…" Arthur continued to struggle to build a sentence.

"I can…what..?" The cat cocked its head. "I can dance? Well, I suppose I do enjoy a good tango. Or a waltz. I'm not great at it, though – I've got four left feet."

Even to Arthur's shocked brain, he could tell that the cat was making fun of him.

"No!" said Arthur. "I mean, you can… you can…"

"Sing?" said the cat. "Well, no, not really. Tried it once. Made a child cry. She thought I was in pain. Very embarrassing."

"No, I mean you can-"

"Read? Oh, I love a good book. Especially if it's about a handsome cat who defeats criminals and eats lots of fish."

"No, you can-"

"Arrange flowers?"

"No, it's that you can-"

"Sew on loose coat buttons?"

"No, you-"

"Sell lemonade out of the back of a manure cart?"

"*Will you stop interrupting me?!*" Arthur suddenly shouted. The cat rested one paw ontop of the other and looked decidedly unimpressed.

"Well, spit it out, then," it said. "I don't have all night."

"You…can…" Arthur breathed slowly, "…*talk!*"

BANGBANGBANG

Straight away, Arthur stiffened with fear. Lady Eris was hammering on her bedroom door from the other end of the hall.

"Arthur Ness! Stop that racket!" she shouted from her doorway. Arthur's door was closed but her voice was so strong and loud, it sounded like she was right there in the room with him. For a moment, not even a talking cat could distract Arthur from how terrified he was of Lady Eris. Just like every time she said his name, he felt cold and hot all at once. Weak kneed and sick in his stomach.

"If I hear another peep out of you," Lady Eris' voice boomed, "I shall hang you from the roof by your shoelaces!"

"Yes, Lady Eris!" Arthur called. "Sorry, Lady Eris!"

Arthur held his breath in silence for a moment and eventually, he could hear Lady Eris' door click shut again.

"Oh, bravo well done," said the cat. "You know, it's a good thing you kept your nerve and didn't tell her I was here."

"Why?" said Arthur returning his gaze to the feline. "Because she'd think I was crazy?"

"No…" The cat yawned then licked its lips. "Because she'd cast a spell and kill us both on the spot. Ooh, nice bed, this."

"Cast a…" Arthur shook his head. "You mean, she's a witch?"

The cat looked up at Arthur, somewhat puzzled. "Couldn't you tell?"

"Stop talking nonsense," Arthur laughed again but was careful to keep his voice low. "Witches aren't *real!*"

The cat looked at Arthur. "You do realise you're conversing with a talking cat?"

"Witches are from fairy tales!"

"Again… talking cat."

Arthur looked around, shaking his head as though he were trying to shake this crazy conversation out of it. He didn't know what to think.

"Do you have a name?" Arthur finally found himself asking.

"Yes, thanks," said the cat, staring around the room.

"…and it is…?"

"None of your business."

"So, what should I call you?"

"Call me what everyone calls me. Call me the Cat."

"Everyone calls you 'the Cat'?" Arthur stood, hands on hips. "Why does everyone call you 'the Cat'? People don't call me 'the Boy'."

"What *do* they call you?"

"Arthur…Arthur Ness."

"Well, Arthur Arthur Ness, unlike you, my name is hidden. Locked away nice and safe where no-one can use it against me. So, in the absence of a name, people call me the Cat. Because I'm a cat. It's really quite simple, even a human should get it…"

Arthur shook his head. "What do you mean, 'use your name against you'? People don't use my name against me!"

"Oh, really?" said the Cat, raising an eyebrow. "Whenever Lady Eris says your name, how do you feel?"

Arthur was about to argue that he didn't feel anything – but then he remembered that he *did* feel something. The weakness, the jelly knees, the hot and cold feeling. The fear.

"But that's…" Arthur stammered, "…that's nothing… I mean, it's not… it's not magic or anything…"

"Do you want proof she's a witch, Arthur Arthur Ness?" The Cat suddenly got up from the bed and strolled over to the open window. "Right-o. Come on, then."

And without another word, it leaped out into the darkness and disappeared. Arthur stood there, his mouth hanging open in shock.

You can't climb out there! You'd fall and break your legs! You don't even like climbing that small tree in your back garden at home!

"Come on out!" the Cat's voice drifted in from the darkness. "It's very easy!"

Arthur looked at the empty window. For a moment, he wondered if anything from the last few minutes had actually happened.

It might all be a dream, Arthur thought. Yes, a strange dream brought about by inhaling too much furniture polish and compost fumes. If he went over to his bed right now and jumped in and closed his eyes tight, it would probably all go away. Yes, Arthur thought, just go to bed. Let it all go away.

But before he knew it, he'd walked not to his bed…

…but to the window.

Okay, he'd take a *little* trip out. He could always wake up later.

He swung his legs out and started the climb down and straight away he found the cat had lied. It wasn't easy. In fact, it was very, very hard. But it immediately became clear that once he'd started, it was easier to go forward than to go back. And before he knew it, his bare feet touched the cold, damp grass.

The cat was sitting there, waiting patiently for him. His green eyes flashed in the dark as he watched Arthur dust himself down.

"Right, Arthur Arthur Ness," he said. "Follow me."

YARNBULLS

The moon was high in the sky as Arthur Ness and the Cat sneaked through the empty lanes and streets of Waterwhistle.

"Keep to the shadows," whispered the Cat as it walked silently ahead of Arthur, "or they'll see you."

There were still some people out and about at this time of night, Arthur saw, though not as many as there would be back in London. Sticking to the shadows as the Cat suggested was the best plan since he didn't want to get told off for being out of bed and sneaking around in his pyjamas.

Although, to tell him off, the villagers would have to actually speak to him. That being the case, he probably didn't have anything to worry about.

"So…" the Cat said as they went along, "Arthur Arthur Ness. It's a bit of a mouthful isn't it?"

"My name isn't Arthur Arthur Ness – it's just Arthur."

"Can I call you Artie?" asked the Cat.

"No."

"Art?"

"No."

"Bob?"

"That's not even my name!"

"Art?"

"You already said that one," Arthur sighed. "And I said no."

"Good grief," said the Cat. "I can tell *you're* going to be hard work."

They carried on in silence for a little while – past Mr Smith's grocer's where Arthur got his compost. Past Mr and Mrs McGugan's sweet shop (which never had anyone in it as far as Arthur could tell). Past Mrs Pettifer's Post Office and Mrs Shepard's garage (Arthur suspected one or both of these ladies had husbands who had gone off to fight in the war – but as no-one spoke to him, he couldn't be sure).

Soon, they both arrived at the village square – the place, Arthur remembered, where Sam's sister, Teresa, had apparently been kidnapped by things no-one could see.

"In here, quickly," said the Cat as it disappeared into a bush. Arthur crawled in behind, flinching every time he thought he saw some kind of creepy-crawly. And there they hid, looking out over the square.

They could see the stone cross in the centre – a memorial, listing the names of all the soldiers that had died in the first World War. Arthur looked quickly away from it and tried not to imagine his father's name being written onto one of those things in the future.

"So…" the Cat said, eventually. "Can you see them?"

Arthur nodded. "Yes. I can see a few people walking about. There's the man who's always walking his dog. So what?"

"Oh, dear."

Arthur frowned. "What?"

"Well, I'm really sorry to have to break it to you," said the Cat very seriously, "but you appear to be a complete and utter dimwit."

"Hey!"

"I'm not talking about the villagers!" scolded the Cat. "Look again!"

"But…what am I looking for?" Arthur asked. But the creature didn't answer. So, Arthur kept looking. And kept seeing nothing.

Eventually, the Cat said, "Are you scared?"

Arthur realised he was shivering – and not entirely from the cold.

"Yes," he admitted, "a bit."

"Well, being scared is okay," said the Cat. "But try to fight your fear. Pretend your fear is like…like a balloon. Give it a punch. It won't pop. But it will wobble."

Arthur shook his head in frustration. It always annoyed him when people said it was okay to be scared. What nonsense! Being scared stopped him from doing things. Things he sometimes really wanted to do. He didn't want to be scared of *anything*. He wanted to be like… like that girl. Sam's sister. What was her name? Teresa.

He wanted to be like Teresa. Yes, Arthur thought, *she* wouldn't be scared. She'd give his stupid fear balloon a punch. He imagined being her and wondered what she'd see if she were here. Would she be able to pick up whatever it was that this silly cat was going on ab-

And that's when Arthur saw it.

It looked like a bull. It had a deep, thick forehead sitting over two, tiny, beady, black eyes. Its neck was super-wide and pulsing with muscles – as was its entire body. It was standing on its hind legs, like a person and it was easily seven feet tall, taller than a doorway. And in its hands, it was holding an axe the size of Arthur himself.

It looked around, silently, menacingly, left and right. Up the village and then back down the other way.

Arthur opened his mouth to shout out *Run! Run for your lives! There's a dangerous creature!* But that's when he noticed something that was even stranger than the beast itself.

Nobody else could see it.

A man walked right by it and didn't so much as glance up at it. An old woman was carrying a basket of something or other. She took a break and put the basket down right in front of the creature's hooved feet. She stood up straight, stretching her back. The bull-thing looked down at her, threateningly. Then she picked up the basket and went along her way, completely oblivious to the creature's presence.

It shifted on its hooves, **clatter**ing them on the cobblestones. And it **snort**ed. Those noises! That was what Arthur had heard before, when he'd been in the shop and when he'd been talking to Sam..! It had been this thing! Standing right next to him, looking down on him and he'd never noticed!

"What... what is it?" Arthur whispered, his mouth completely dry.

"It's called a Yarnbull," said the Cat, quietly. "And I'm afraid the bad news is… it isn't alone."

Arthur looked again and his eyes opened wide in shock. He could see them. He could actually see them.

Loads of Yarnbulls.

Dotted all over the village. Some were holding axes, some had swords. They were stood still or they were striding up and down the streets and lanes. Some alone, some in pairs. But they were all completely fearsome and terrifying. And they were watching the villagers.

Very closely.

"How come…" Arthur struggled for breath, "…how come nobody can see them?"

"They're too scared," replied the Cat. "It's the perfect way to control people. Make them so scared, they forget there's anything out there controlling them in the first place."

"But what are they doing here?"

"They're guards."

"What are they guarding?"

"They're here to make sure nobody cuts the Threads."

"Threads..?" Arthur was confused. "What threads?"

The Cat looked up at Arthur, quizzically, "Can't you see them?"

"Are… are they big?" Arthur asked.

Now it was the Cat's turn to be confused, "How can you see the Yarnbulls but not the Threads?"

"I don't know," said Arthur, getting a little annoyed. "You're the talking cat showing me the armed bulls, you tell *me!*"

The Cat didn't say anything. He looked at Arthur as though he was trying to figure something out.

"Are they here all the time?" Arthur asked, eventually. "The Yarnbulls?"

"Oh, yes," said the Cat. "*All* the time."

"Where do they come from?"

The Cat fixed its green eyes on Arthur. "What do you think you've been growing in the garden for Lady Eris?"

"Th..*those things?*" Arthur couldn't believe it. "I've been growing *those things?* But… there's nothing in the garden. It's empty!"

"No, it just *looks* empty," said the Cat. "Because, as you can see, they're good at staying hidden. But trust me. That garden's *full* of them."

Arthur looked back at the village, back at the Yarnbulls all over the square and the surrounding roads. No wonder this place was so silent. Everyone was petrified. And they didn't even know it.

"When she first got here, months ago," the Cat said, "Lady Eris put the village under her control. The Yarnbulls are here to make sure it stays that way."

"But, how did she control everyone in the first place?"

"She Bound them."

"Bound?" Arthur said, a little puzzled. "You mean, like, tied-up?"

"Yep," the Cat nodded. "With the Threads."

Arthur sighed, frustrated. The Threads, again.

"But..." Arthur looked back out toward the village, puzzled, "...no-one's tied up."

"You can see the Yarnbulls because you forced yourself to be a little bit brave," the Cat encouraged. "The Threads follow the same rules. Go on, try again."

Arthur shook his head, a growing sense of defeat beginning to build ominously in his belly. "Sorry... I still can't see them..."

"Well, they *are* harder to see," the Cat admitted. "The Yarnbulls are a real danger so, if you try, you can see them quite easily. But the Threads are a very clever kind of danger. And all clever kinds of danger are hard to spot."

Arthur suddenly started feeling more and more angry. Why could he not make himself more brave? He could see the Yarnbulls – why not the Threads? Why did he always fail when it came to being brave? He just wanted to scream at the top of his lungs… but, of course, he was too scared. The Cat didn't miss Arthur's growing frustration.

"Listen, Arthur, I need your help," it said. "It's okay to be scared, but-"

"*Stop saying that!*" Arthur had to force himself not to shout. "It's *not* okay! *You* try it, sometime!"

"Arthur, listen-"

But Arthur didn't want to listen. He scrambled out of the bush and without even dusting himself down, he ran all the way back to the house. Keeping to the shadows, Arthur kept out of the way of the Yarnbulls… but as he ran, he noticed that, actually, he couldn't see them anymore.

Of course not. You heard the Cat. Only brave people can see them.
Just because you pretended to be Teresa, that doesn't make you brave.
You don't have any bravery of your own –
you had to borrow someone else's.

Arthur got all the way across the village, up the lane and back to the garden of the big house and, of course, could see no Yarnbulls growing there at all. He looked up and saw his bedroom light was still on. His bed. An escape from this madness. He took a step toward it – and almost went sprawling to the ground as he tripped over the Cat, which had appeared out of nowhere.

"You think you're the only person who gets scared?" the small, black creature said, its eyes flashing an angry green. "Look at all those people out there! They're so scared, they can't see the Yarnbulls at all!"

"Yes!" Arthur scrunched his hands into fists. "Because Lady Eris has Bound them! That's what you said!

Cast some spell on them! But what's *my* excuse, eh? She hasn't cast any spells on me! And do you know why not? Because she doesn't have to! I'm *already scared!*"

"Arthur, I need you," said the Cat. "I need your help. There are things I have to do and I can't do them without you."

"Well, I'm sorry to have to break it to you," Arthur said, a stinging feeling building behind his eyes, "but you're a dimwit. Because out of all the people you could have picked, you've gone and chosen the most useless person in the world!"

The Cat stared at Arthur for a long while, never blinking. Then it shook its head.

"Maybe I am a dimwit," it said. "Maybe I'm getting old. Used up too many lives. I'm starting to make stupid decisions. Fine. Go to bed. Go to sleep. And when you wake up, convinced this was all a dream, then you'll go back to how you were before. Too scared to see the Yarnbulls. But at least you'll be safe from them. Yes, Lady Eris will control you like she's controlling the entire village. But it'll be okay. Because, like them, you won't even know she's doing it."

And with that, the Cat turned and disappeared into the night.

Arthur stared into the darkness for a moment, feeling colder and smaller and more alone than he'd felt in a long time.

Eventually, tired and drained, he turned towards Lady Eris' house and headed for the drainpipe that would take him back to his room and his bed.

SCARED AGAIN

The next day went in a bit of a blur.

Arthur scrubbed the kitchen floor, polished the silver in the front room, fetched some more compost from the village, dusted some cobwebs from the ceiling in the hallway, brought the coal in from the shed and a dozen other back-breaking, mind-numbing tasks. And all the time, the idea of talking cats, Yarnbulls and Lady Eris being a witch seemed like the most absurd nonsense ever.

Polishing the door knobs to all the downstairs rooms, Arthur thought about Sam and his foolish stories. Silly tales made up by a bored child. And everything that had seemed strange actually had a simple explanation when he thought about it logically:

1) The snorting and scraping noises Arthur had heard were just from all those animals that these crazy people had walking around their village. (Almost certainly, it was the cows. Arthur did not like the cows).

2) It wasn't a witch's spell that made the villagers not speak to each other. The reason was simple; they were just rude.

3) Then of course, all this led to him having such a lucid dream last night. It had been vivid, he'd admit that. It felt very real. He could still feel the icy fear of seeing those Yarnbulls. But a vivid dream is still just a dream.

4) And then there was the cat. A talking cat, no less. Arthur wasn't overly fond of cats so it made sense that his fear of living in Waterwhistle should manifest itself in his dreams as a black cat. To lead him out of normality and into craziness. To keep calling him 'Arthur Arthur Ness'.

Arthur suddenly found himself grinning.

It was such a silly joke – Arthur Arthur Ness – and yet, strangely… it *did* make him feel a little better to think of it. Yes, it had certainly all been a strange, fantastical dream. And yet, Arthur found himself wishing that the talking cat, at least, was real.

The door handle Arthur was now polishing had a stubborn stain on it. He gave it an extra hard rub and

click

the handle pushed down and the door drifted open an inch. Only then did Arthur realise that the doorknob he was cleaning was actually on the door that led to the drawing room. So now, in front of him stood a thin, vertical-strip view of the place he had first been forbidden to go.

His initial thought was to quickly pull the door closed again before Lady Eris came down and caught him. His second thought was to push it open and take a look inside.

Unbelievably, he went with his second thought.

The door glided open silently and Arthur peeked his head round. The room was large with a high ceiling, just like the other downstairs rooms he'd been cleaning. But he didn't much care about the wallpaper or the carpets or the chairs.

Arthur wanted to get a look at the tapestry.

The wall-mounted woven rug was *huge*. It went from the floor right to the ceiling and seemed to stretch almost as wide as the room itself. It was kind of old and dirty, Arthur thought. It reminded him of the worn-out rug in the hallway back home. Obviously that was a lot smaller than this – and it was meant to be walked on rather than looked at – but they both had pictures woven into the fabric.

Arthur was a lot closer to the tapestry now than he was on the night he arrived and he could see the pictures on it very clearly. There were lots of little islands – floating islands, hanging in space. The threadwork was so intricate, you could even see little people on the floating chunks of land.

The islands were all connected to each other by hundreds and hundreds of little, black lines that criss-crossed all over the picture like some kind of gigantic spider's web.

Arthur's eyes opened wide with wonder. This thing was *amazing*. Who had made it, he wondered? How long ago? What for? Arthur knew, somehow, that this thing hadn't belonged to Lord and Lady Roberts. It had definitely been Lady Eris who had brought it into the house.

Arthur thought that maybe somewhere deep down, he'd wanted to look at this tapestry because he thought there might be something special about it. Magical, even. But now he could see it properly, he could see that, impressive as it was, it was nevertheless just a big piece of fancy material. Seeing the cat on it before, thinking it had moved... it had all just been a trick of the light. A result of his exhausted, homesick mind.

Strangely enough, though, as Arthur cast his eyes up and down the tapestry, he couldn't see the picture of the cat anywhere. It had to be here somewhere…

Creeeeek

Arthur's breath caught in his throat – the top step!

Lady Eris!

Barely daring to even breath, Arthur darted out of the room, pulled the door shut and went back to polishing the handle. After a few seconds, he realised Lady Eris wasn't coming down the stairs after all. It must have just been the old, wooden house making noises on its own, the way old, wooden houses do.

Breathing a sigh of relief, Arthur scolded himself.

Keep your nose out of things, scaredy-cat!
There's nothing going on! Do as you're told!

He hadn't seen the picture of the cat on the tapestry, but Arthur knew it must be on there somewhere. And it explained why he'd dreamed of a cat – because he remembered seeing it on the tapestry on his first night.

All in all, the young Londoner knew that nothing strange was going on in the house or in the village. Last night was just a fantasy, created by his own mind. There was no magic, no witch, no bull creatures, no talking cat and definitely, definitely no spark of bravery from Arthur.

He finished with the polishing and headed outside.

He still had compost to spread.

STILL SCARED BUT...

It was while spreading his fourth shovel-load of compost when the thought suddenly struck Arthur.

Threads!

The word suddenly felt like it was emblazoned across his brain, like he could see it written in huge, firey letters in the dull, late afternoon sky.

1. On the tapestry – little islands, connected by threads.
2. The villagers bound by invisible threads.
3. Yarnbulls – yarn, being a type of thread.
4. Arthur remembered being close to Lady Eris' face on that first night and thinking that her hair did look like lots of threads.
5. Even the tapestry itself – a huge picture made of threads.

Lots of things to do with threads. Co-incidence?

Or something more?

What are you still thinking about this for?
I thought you'd realised it was all in your head!

Something made Arthur suddenly look up at the house. At Lady Eris' bedroom window.

There she was, staring down at him. Just for a moment.

Then her face disappeared behind the curtains again.

Arthur looked around him, around the garden. Could there be dozens of Yarnbulls here, right now? Growing out of the ground?

Of course not, don't be stupid.

What if…what if he tried to be brave right now? Would he see them?

Go on, then. Try it. I dare you.

No, he couldn't see anything. Maybe he wasn't brave enough. Or maybe, he was stopping himself being brave on purpose. After all, last night, he'd forced himself to be a tiny bit brave and had seen the Yarnbulls for a moment. But it had scared him so much, his bravery had vanished again and the creatures were hidden from sight once more. He'd even managed to convince himself that they weren't real.

Last night was a dream, *stupid! Stop thinking about this stuff!*

And that was the problem, Arthur realised. The villagers were all scared so none of them saw the Yarnbulls. And that kept them safe. If you happened to be brave enough to see them – like Teresa was – then the Yarnbulls would come after you.

Being brave enough to *see* the danger meant you were *in* danger.

…stop it…stop thinking about this nonsense…get back to your work…
…please…?

But, Arthur wasn't just like the villagers, was he? They were scared mostly because of the Binding spell that Lady Eris was casting on them (Arthur suddenly wondered if that's what his host's strange 'dancing' had been all about). The magic was helping keep the villagers scared but what about Arthur? She hadn't bothered with him, had she? The only thing keeping Arthur scared...

...was himself.

"Arthur Ness."

The thin, sharp voice made Arthur jump. He hadn't even heard Lady Eris come outside and here she suddenly was beside him. He looked up at her, fearfully.

"I am going into the village," she said. "I will not be long. I want this entire garden done by the time I get back."

"Yes, Lady Eris."

The tall, thin woman cast her raven-dark eyes down over Arthur Ness and just for a second, a cruel, self-satisfied smirk crossed her lips. Then she turned on her heel and left, heading out towards the village lane.

Arthur replayed that smile in his mind. He knew what it meant. It meant that Lady Eris was pleased with herself for guessing that Arthur would do as he was told. That he would be too scared to cause her any trouble.

She was pleased for being right.

The smile replayed itself over and over in Arthur's mind and he felt something that surprised him. A sudden urge. An urge to show her she was *wrong*.

Show her?

No, not her.

Show *himself*.

... but you can't...

Yes. He could.

He threw the spade down into the soil and ran as fast as he could into the house and straight towards Lady Eris' room.

A FLASH OF BRAVERY

Arthur sprinted all the way through the hallway, up the stairs, along the landing and burst into Lady Eris room in just a few seconds.

His heart was beating hard in his chest and his head felt a little woozy – but not from the run. It was from the fear. Fear of what he was daring to do. But, for the first time in his life, the fear felt a little different. It was more like... *excitement*.

The first time in his life? Actually, no. He had felt it once before, just a teeny, tiny bit. Last night, when he'd climbed out of his window after the Cat.

Still, he had no time to waste marvelling at his newfound bravery, however brief it might turn out to be. He had come in here for a specific reason. After all, if Lady Eris really was a witch and really was binding the villagers with invisible threads, then what would be her biggest fear?

Well, thought Arthur, it was quite simple. Her biggest fear would be the villagers *seeing* the threads. Teresa had seen what was going on. That's why the Yarnbulls had kidnapped her. If the villagers were somehow shown what was happening, the fear might disappear. And Lady Eris would be powerless.

Arthur might have thought that there was no way to make the threads visible if not for one thing he had happened to see by chance yesterday. A mirror in a safe. Because why else would Lady Eris be keeping it locked away unless it could cause her trouble?

Immediately, Arthur ran across the room and put his hand on the safe door handle. What if it was locked? This would all just be a waste of time. He might even get caught and it would all be for nothing.

Yes… just let go of the handle and get back to the garden.
If you leave now, Lady Eris need never know
you came up here.

The thought of Lady Eris coming back and finding Arthur exactly where she left him and smirking again at how easily she had controlled him… Arthur shook his head and the urge of defiance flooded into his body again. He twisted the handle and pulled…

The safe door opened.

This showed how confident Lady Eris was that Arthur's fear would keep him in line. She knew he'd seen the safe and yet she hadn't even bothered to lock it!

Arthur reached inside. The mirror handle felt cold against his fingers. He took it out and looked at it properly for the first time.

It was beautiful! The handle was silver and ivory and lead up to a gold-framed mirror. The glass had a strange, unearthly sheen to it. Different colours danced across its surface as Arthur tilted it back and forth. And all around the edge of the mirror were carvings and incriptions in a language Arthur couldn't even recognise, let alone read.

SLAM!

That was the back door. Lady Eris was back, already!

Quick as he could, Arthur stuffed the mirror into the front waistband of his shorts and pulled his jumper over the protruding handle. He ran out into the hall and no sooner had he silently closed the bedroom door than Lady Eris appeared at the top of the stairs.

She looked at Arthur with dark, distrustful eyes.

"What are you doing up here, Arthur Ness?"

Again, Arthur felt the cold weakness come over him. He had to fight every urge to simply drop to his knees and confess everything.

"I was just…I was just…"

Just what? Think fast, scaredy-cat.

"I was just going to clean the hallway again," Arthur said, suddenly. "I trampled compost in here from the garden."

Lady Eris climbed up the final step and moved slowly towards Arthur, her eyes never leaving his. It felt like she was doing that thing again, thought Arthur, flicking through the pages of his brain, looking for something.

The mirror slipped a little bit in his shorts. Arthur tried hard not to sweat.

Please don't fall out…*please*…

Then, Lady Eris simply walked past Arthur and off towards her room.

"Finish in the garden, Arthur Ness," she said without looking back. And she closed the door behind her.

Breathing a sigh of relief, Arthur reached into his shorts and pulled out the mirror. Then, without waiting even one more second, he ran downstairs as fast as his legs could carry him.

THE MIRROR

Arthur didn't stop running when he got to the bottom of the stairs. He didn't stop running when he got out of the house. He didn't even stop running when he got to the garden and was shocked to see several Yarnbull horns peeking up through the soil.

He kept running all the way down the lane towards the village, his hand on the front of his jumper, the mirror hidden underneath.

Arthur did finally stop running, however, when he got to the village and saw something that, even though he'd prepared himself for it, still sent shivers of fear throughout his body.

Yarnbulls. Everywhere.

There were even more than last night – or maybe he could just see more than he could last night. Back then, he'd pretended to be Teresa and tried to use some of her bravery. Today, he was just being himself. And all the bravery he'd managed to gather together was now in danger of seeping away as he watched the huge beasts strolling about the village.

But none of them made a move toward him. *They don't realise*, Arthur had to remind himself. *They don't know I can see them.*

And so, with a deep breath and a marshalling of his nerves, Arthur walked as slowly and calmly through the middle of the village – and the middle of the Yarnbulls – as he could.

He tried to keep himself as casual as possible. He walked past Yarnbull after Yarnbull, each time keeping his gaze facing forwards, doing his best to ignore the huge creatures as they watched him go past. He could feel the hotness of their gaze on him as he walked. Watching him, watching all the villagers for any sign that they weren't as scared as they should be. But Arthur kept his cool. He made himself seem just like the rest of them – completely unaware of the monsters standing about on the perfectly green village lawns.

Eventually, Arthur made it to the village square and, checking no-one was watching him, ducked down behind the bush next to the bin. It was the same bush that he and the Cat had shared the night before.

Taking a deep breath, Arthur took the mirror out. Time to find out if this really was something special.

He looked into it. All Arthur saw at first was his own face. He turned it slightly so he could see over his shoulder and get more of the village behind him. And his heart almost stopped.

Everything was absolutely *covered* in threads. It was like a cotton factory had exploded and thrown reels of the stuff everywhere. Fine, black strands cris-crossed all over the place, connecting everything to everything else. They covered roofs and streetlamps and shop fronts. They wrapped up gardens and gates and entire cars. They even went into the ground and came back up wrapped around the carrots and turnips growing in Mr. Babbage's yard. And then Arthur saw Mr. Babbage himself. He had to put his hand over his mouth to stop himself crying out in shock.

Mr. Babbage was almost completely enveloped in threads. His entire head was wrapped up like an Egyptian mummy in tight, black wrappings. Eyes, nose, mouth, all covered. It was the same with parts of his body and hands. And yet, he was moving around, working in his garden, completely unaware there was anything wrong.

But if his eyes were covered, Arthur thought, surely he couldn't see anything at all. Yet, there he was, sprinkling water on his vegetables and picking out weeds that were poking up from between the plants.

Arthur looked away from the mirror glanced over at the old man with his own eyes. Nothing. No threads at all. Completely normal. He looked back into Mr Babbage's reflection in the mirror and there they were. Threads, all over the man's face and arms and hands and covering his eyes.

Maybe what the old man was seeing, Arthur thought, was just *like* real life… without actually *being* real life.

Arthur looked from person to person in the reflection of the mirror and it was the same with them all. All tied up. And not a single one of them knew it.

So this was what the Cat had meant, Arthur realised. This was being Bound.

The entire village was caught up in a giant spider's web of threads and all the strands rose up into the sky and headed off eventually into one direction. They coalesced and joined together at a single point of origin. And that single point was the big house. The turret on the corner.

Lady Eris' room.

"Scary, isn't it?"

Arthur nearly jumped out of his skin at the sound of the Cat's voice.

"Don't do that!" he breathed as he glanced down at the small, black creature, appearing from nowhere.

"So," said the Cat, "you fought your fear, realised the mirror was important, sneaked into Lady Eris' room, grabbed it and came out here to see what it could show you. Not bad for the most useless person in the world. And you did it all without any action music!"

"Action music?"

"You know," said the Cat, "like in the movies. The music you imagine in your head when you have to do heroic and awesome action stuff! Doesn't everyone do that?"

Arthur stared at him, blankly.

"Okay…" said the Cat, returning his gaze to the villagers, "…just me, then…"

"Every single person's been Bound," Arthur said, looking into the mirror, again. "Everyone but me."

"And that," said the Cat, "is exactly why it's down to you to do something about it."

Arthur felt his head swimming as the situation began to sink in. The bit of bravery he'd managed to grab onto was, even now, melting in his hands like a sliver of ice, "But…but, what good can I do? Lady Eris hasn't Bound me because she knows I don't pose any threat. She knows I'm worthless."

"Ah, well, she's already wrong, isn't she?"

"What do you mean?"

The Cat locked eyes with Arthur. "*Nobody's* worthless."

Arthur felt a little numb. Could the Cat be right? Arthur had managed to get this far by stealing the mirror. Now he'd started, could it be like clinging onto the side of the house after following the Cat out the window – easier to go on than go back?

Uncertain, Arthur looked into the mirror again.

And saw a Yarnbull raising its axe towards him.

"Move!" yelled the Cat.

Arthur dived to the ground and the massive axe whistled past his ear, missing him by millimetres and **CRASH**ed into the bin next to them, smashing it into smithereens with a single blow.

Arthur lay on the ground, looking up at the biggest, most fierce creature he had ever seen. The creature, all snarls and anger and bared teeth, raised its axe over its head once more. And the Cat said, "I'm not sure, but I think we might have been discovered."

YARNBULL CHASE

Arthur rolled to one side as the Yarnbull's axe flew down again. With an almighty **THUD**, it embedded itself into the ground, Arthur on one side of it, the Cat on the other.

The creature grunted and hefted the huge, metal weapon back into the air a third time. Without thinking, Arthur grabbed a handful of soil and threw it into the Yarnbull's beady eyes. It howled in rage and staggered back for a moment, taken by surprise.

"Run!" yelled the Cat.

And run, they did.

In seconds, the pair were out from behind the bush and off across the village square, the Cat in front, Arthur sprinting as fast as he could behind. All Arthur could hear was the **boom Boom BOOM** of the Yarnbull's hooves as it pounded the ground in pursuit. Then came its snorting. And its deafening **ROAR**.

Arthur thought it sounded very angry. But then he suddenly realised it wasn't just bellowing in anger.

It was calling for help.

"Look out!" cried the Cat as three more Yarnbulls crashed out of a side-lane and onto the main road, ahead of the fleeing pair, forcing them to skid to a halt.

"Help!" Arthur cried out to the passing villagers. "Somebody, please, help us!"

A couple of passers-by glanced up at them but they soon turned away, completely disinterested.

"It's no use!" the Cat shouted. "They can't see them!"

Four Yarnbulls now surrounded the pair and began closing in, snarling and brandishing their weapons.

"This way!" the Cat suddenly cried out. He ran straight towards one of them and disappeared in between its legs. Arthur felt a sudden, freezing flush at the thought of doing what the Cat had just done. And yet, off he ran, straight towards the same Yarnbull.

With a deafening bellow, the creature raised its sword towards Arthur and brought it down with pulverising force – but Arthur was no longer there. He'd already skidded through, in between the creature's legs after the Cat.

There was no time to congratulate himself, though, as Arthur followed the tiny, black shape.

"Don't dawdle, Arthur!" the Cat yelled back as he ran. "It's not just a haircut they're trying to give you!"

Howling with bloodcurdling fury, the Yarnbulls pounded after the pair.

"Where are we going?" Arthur cried out as he ran.

"Back to the house!"

"WHAT?! Back to the place where the Yarnbulls actually *come* from?!"

"It's the only way out!"

"Out? Out where?"

But the Cat didn't answer, he just kept running. Hearing the Yarnbulls getting closer, Arthur thought running was probably the best idea right now. Talking could wait.

And so they ran, all the way back up the lane and towards the big house. Somehow, short, fast legs managed to keep ahead of long, slow ones. Within moments, they were dashing through the garden. As fast as they could, they weaved in and out of the Yarnbull heads and horns that were poking through the ground.

With a cry of fright, Arthur dodged past one Yarnbull head that roared and snapped massive teeth at him. Luckily, with the rest of its body still buried in the earth, roaring was all it could do.

Finally, they reached the house. Quick as a flash, the Cat was through the kitchen window. Arthur crashed into the back door. He flung it open, ran through, slammed it behind him and ducked as a massive axe smashed it to pieces. Arthur ran past the window as another Yarnbull shattered it, reaching massive arms in for him.

Arthur ducked the creature's monstrously large hands (with fingers each as thick as Arthur's wrist) and ran after the Cat out of the kitchen, into the hallway and along the corridor – only then realising where the Cat was taking them.

The drawing room.

Bursting in, the first thing Arthur noticed was the tapestry.

The second thing he noticed was Lady Eris.

The third thing he noticed was the fact that Lady Eris was floating in mid-air.

In shock, Arthur dropped the mirror (he was mildly surprised to realise he was still holding it) and it skidded across the floor, stopping face up in the middle of the room.

"So, it appears I was mistaken about you, Arthur Ness," Lady Eris said, looking down at him. The Cat was nowhere to be seen. "You have proven to be a problem after all."

Arthur looked down at the mirror and saw Lady Eris' reflection. He was surprised to see she wasn't actually floating at all. She was being held aloft by masses and masses of threads that emanated from her body and ran to every corner of the room, attached to the walls and ceiling. Many of them ran out through the windows and off into the village. The Cat had been right – all the threads Binding the villagers were coming directly from her.

Then Arthur caught a glimpse of the tapestry's reflection in the mirror too and he saw something he literally couldn't believe.

The tapestry wasn't a tapestry.

It was a doorway.

Suddenly, there was a deafening scuffle as the four Yarnbulls reached the entrance to the drawing room. Lady Eris looked toward them for just a second. And, in that second, Arthur ran towards the tapestry, knowing instinctively that this is what the Cat had wanted them to do.

"Not so fast, Arthur Ness."

Something whipped its way toward Arthur and wrapped itself around his wrist. A black thread held him tight.

A cruel grin wrapped itself around Lady Eris' face and the sheer evil in that smile sent waves of terror crashing through Arthur's body. She started reeling him in, hand over hand, like a terrified fish. The Yarnbulls, mean-faced, waited at the door and silently watched their mistress as she prepared to put an end to this troublesome situation.

Arthur could hear the voice in his head getting ready to tell him what a failure he was…

All of a sudden, a black shape flew out of nowhere and landed on the black thread connecting Arthur to the witch.

The Cat was back.

"*You!*" Lady Eris stopped still in shock. And now, for the first time, Arthur saw something on her face he never thought he would ever see. *Fear.* He couldn't quite believe it.

Lady Eris was *terrified* of the Cat.

"What are *you* doing here?!" she screeched. "You were dead!"

"I was." The Cat agreed. "But I got better. Here, Arthur, let me give you a hand. Sorry, a paw."

And with that, the Cat swiped a single claw at the thread and snapped it cleanly in two – Arthur was free!

Seeing the boy get free, the Yarnbulls suddenly sprang to life again and squeezed through the doorway, one after the other. Once again, Arthur ran towards the tapestry.

"Wait, the mirror!" Arthur saw it resting against some spare sweeping brushes. He reached a hand towards it but then pulled back at the last second as a huge Yarnbull hoof slammed down onto the floor and smashed the intricate glass and ivory to pieces.

"It's okay, leave it!" the Cat yelled.

Arthur had no choice but to do what the Cat said and he put his head down and ran towards the tapestry as fast as he could. All he had time to think was – *if this isn't really a doorway, this is really going to hurt…*

Arthur opened his eyes.

He was in a castle.

A *castle.*

"I really hope this is the last surprise of the day," Arthur said breathlessly, "because I honestly don't think I can take any more…"

His gaze ran over the many tapestries hanging on the stone walls, the suits of armour dotted about, the great, long banqueting table in the middle of the room… And on the wall he had just emerged from, another huge tapestry, identical to the one they'd just run through.

"Where…where are we?" Arthur asked.

"Escape first, questions later!" the Cat shouted as he darted past.

"Arthur Ness!" came Lady Eris' scream as she emerged from the gate-tapestry. Once again, Arthur felt that hot-cold feeling come over him as his knees began to turn to rubber.

"Come along, Artie!" the Cat yelled as it disappeared off towards an exit doorway. "Less gawping, more running!"

And so, witch and terror-creatures at his heel, Arthur Ness ran. And ran. And ran…

And very soon, he found himself standing at the edge of a cliff – black space at his back, the Cat at his side, a mysterious cable attached to the ground by his feet, Lady Eris and her creatures in front of him… and nowhere to run.

And that's just when the cable attached to the ground began to shake and shake and shake.

A loud **whoosh**ing noise blasted down from above them and Arthur looked up. With wide eyes, he immediately realised that running through a tapestry and finding himself in a castle was *not* going to be the last big surprise of the day.

A galleon – an actual, actual pirate ship – came hurtling down out of the black sky. It's black and red sails billowed, full of air and aggression. An anchor chain trailed from the underside of the ship and attached it to the cable with a huge, metal ring. As the vessel flew down toward the ground, the anchor-ring ran along the cable, making it shake, violently and filling the air with a loud, continuous **thrumm**.

"I know you wanted us to stop for a bit of a gossip, Eris," the Cat said, jumping up onto Arthur's shoulder, "but my taxi has arrived and I really can't keep it waiting. You wouldn't believe how much extra they charge for daring rescues. Seriously, it's just ridiculous."

The end of a rope came tumbling over the side of the ship and Arthur instinctively grabbed hold of it with both hands.

"But don't you worry, Eris…" the Cat's voice was suddenly firm, serious and scary, "…we'll be back."

And the ship swung round in a great spiral and shot back up the cable, pulling the rope tight and then up into the air. Arthur cried out as the ground suddenly disappeared from beneath his feet. They were pulled along at breakneck speed and as they flew up and away from the castle, Arthur could finally see the whole island.

It looked just like the islands on the tapestry back in the house. Floating in the black nothingness. And, just like the pictures on the tapestry, there were more cables coming from the island and going off in other directions.

But, as fast as they were going, the island was soon gone. Swallowed by the darkness.

That was it. They'd escaped!

"Come on!" the Cat called into Arthur's ear over the deafening howl of rushing wind and the thrumming of the anchor-ring. "Best get ourselves aboard. You don't want to fall into the NothingSpace. Trust me, that's a fate infinitely worse than death."

Without even stopping to ask just what kind of fate could be infinitely worse than death, Arthur started to pull himself hand over hand towards the ship.

As soon as they got within an arm's length of the side, the Cat jumped off Arthur's shoulder and landed lightly on the side-rails. And within moments, Arthur had hauled himself aboard and tumbled down onto the wooden deck.

"Permission to come aboard, Captain," he heard the Cat say, the familiar grin in his voice. Arthur looked up. He'd expected to see loads of sailors or pirates or soldiers all over the deck. But all there was to greet them was a single person.

A girl, about his own age.

"Wow, Cat, that were close!" she said. "I were beginning to think you weren't goin' to turn up!"

"Well, Arthur and I had a little bit of trouble with almost being chopped to pieces," said the Cat. "I do apologise."

The girl smiled at Arthur and held out a hand. She looked familiar, but Arthur couldn't quite place it...

"Nice to meet you, Arthur Ness. Welcome to Arilon," she grinned. "Welcome aboard the *Gallopin' Snake*."

And with that smile, Arthur *did* recognise her. It was the same smile that Sam had when he'd first met him.

"Teresa!" Arthur babbled. "You're Teresa Smith!"

Teresa's eyebrows raised a little in surprise.

"That's me. And let me tell you," she smiled a dark, daring smile. "If you thought this were all about a few Yarnbulls in Waterwhistle, you haven't seen *nothin'* yet..."

THREAD TWO

ARILON

THE QUEEN

There's a ship called the *Twilight Palace* and it sails through the black NothingSpace, moving along the Travel Lines between islands. And it never stops. Never once pausing for supplies or food or rest or repair. Sleeplessly, it prowls the empty space between the islands.

People everywhere – sailors and landfolk alike – sit around campfires or at tables in taverns or in the safety of their homes at night and they whisper in hushed tones about the Nightmare Ship. What kind of vessel never needs to stop for repairs? What kind of crew never needs to sleep?

Few people have been aboard the *Twilight Palace* and come back to tell the tale. So, people know very little about the vessel at all.

The only thing they really know is that the *Twilight Palace* – the Nightmare Ship – is the home of the monarch of Arilon. The terrible and frightening ruler of the islands and the sun and the NothingSpace between them.

The *Twilight Palace* is the home of the Queen.

And it's aboard this ship that Lady Eris now finds herself.

Captain Isaac knocks on the door of the Royal Chamber.

"Yes?" comes a voice from within.

"Lady Eris has arrived, your Grace."

"Send her in, Captain."

The Captain, firm and tall (though not as tall as Lady Eris) opens the door and stands to one side. The Noir Lady steps inside and the door is closed softly behind her.

As usual, the Queen's chamber is in near-darkness. This is something Lady Eris is always grateful for. It means she can't see the eyes that stare at her from the walls.

The throne, a golden chair covered in fine, woven silk, sits empty and alone at the far end of the room. The Queen very rarely uses it. Instead, Lady Eris finds her in her favoured position; sitting cross-legged on the floor in the centre of the chambers, her robes splayed out on the floor around her.

In her hands is a small, cloth doll, finely embroidered, onto which the Queen is sewing a leg. Around her, as usual, spread out all over the throne room floor are more silk dolls. Hundreds of them. They are of all sizes and all types. Dolls of men and women, children and the elderly. Dolls of soldiers, dolls of beggars, dolls of kings and queens and dolls of pirates.

Lady Eris knows better than to interrupt the Queen when she is sewing. She waits. All the while, unblinking eyes in the wall continue to stare at her.

Eventually, her gaze still fixed on the doll in her hands, the Queen speaks in a low, rich voice.

"We have a problem, Lady Eris."

"Yes, your Grace."

"The Cat has returned," the Queen says, sewing on. "The Cat whom we had thought finally destroyed."

"Yes, your Grace," Lady Eris says again.

"The human boy is with him."

Lady Eris shakes her head. "Arthur Ness is of no consequence, your Grace. He is weak. Fearful. He is no longer under my roof but he is, as ever, under my control."

"You are so confident, Lady Eris?" the Queen sounds strangely amused. "You do not think the boy will feel braver now he has escaped your clutches?"

"I am sure he *will* feel braver," Lady Eris says. "Still, he will be of no consequence."

"Let us hope you are right, Lady Eris."

Lady Eris doesn't reply and the pair remain in silence for a few moments more. The Queen continues to sew her doll with long, smooth strokes of fine, silver thread.

"How much does he know about us?" she asks eventually. "The boy?"

"I am sure the Cat will inform him of all he needs to know," says Lady Eris.

Then a horrid sound erupts from the Queen – the dark sound of her laughter.

"He will fill the child's head with lies. That has always been the Cat's way." The Queen speaks while her gaze remains fixed on her doll. "The only truths the child will get are the ones the Cat wishes him to have."

Lady Eris takes a deep breath. "In any event, your Grace, Arthur Ness is aware of what I am doing to the inhabitants of Waterwhistle."

"But he does not know why?"

"He does not." Lady Eris reassures her Queen. "And I am confident that the Cat also remains unaware of our true goal."

Silence again. The Queen continues to sew.

Lady Eris glances at one of the walls for a moment and glimpses the eyes. And the faces. And the long, thin bodies. The eyes continue to stare at her with envy and hatred. She looks quickly away.

The Queen draws the thread through the doll one final time. Then she raises it to her mouth and bites the thread, snapping it. (For a second, Lady Eris glimpses the jewels in the Queen's teeth).

The monarch gracefully slides the needle - elaborate gold and emerald - into her robes. Then she places the doll delicately on the edge of a nearby table.

Lady Eris contains her surprise as she realises that she recognises the doll's face.

"You will return to Waterwhistle," the Queen says, looking only at her newest doll. "The human village is key to our plans. The machine grows more complete every day. It is of utmost importance that you attain full and complete control over Waterwhistle and its inhabitants as soon as possible. If even one of them is capable of a single act of bravery, if even one of them can see the Threads or the Yarnbulls..." Her eyes rest on the doll of a little girl and her voice grows quiet, as if talking to herself. "...all could be lost..."

Lady Eris nods, slowly. "And what of Arthur Ness? And the Cat?"

"You will send agents to locate them," the Queen replies, still not looking at Lady Eris. Instead, her gaze floats over her dolls, landing on one after another after another. "When they have been found, you shall return to Arilon and deal with matters personally."

"Yes, your Grace...but..."

"What is it, Lady Eris?"

"I dare not rely on Yarnbulls alone for this. They are nothing but mindless brutes. I need something more... subtle."

The Queen is looking, now, at a doll by her feet. It's a doll of an old woman with bound hands and feet. A dark smile flits across the Queen's mouth.

"I thought Arthur Ness was to be of no consequence..?" Her voice is ever-so-slightly mocking.

"Yes, your Grace," replies Lady Eris. "But it is better to be prudent. To be prepared. We must give them no chance to ruin our plans."

Finally and for the first time, the Queen raises her eyes towards Lady Eris. The Noir Lady is momentarily taken aback, as she always is. The Queen's dark red eyes bore into Lady Eris in a manner not unlike the way Lady Eris' eyes would bore into Arthur Ness. It sends chills through the Noir Lady's body and she wishes silently that the Queen would look elsewhere. But she keeps her tongue silent and forces herself to return the gaze.

"You wish to awaken the Needlemen?" the Queen asks, slowly, deliberately.

Lady Eris nods. "Yes. If it pleases your Grace."

The Queen continues to stare at Lady Eris. Between her eyes and the eyes in the wall, Lady Eris can barely stand it. But it will be worth it...as long as she says-

"Very well. The Needlemen are yours to command."

Lady Eris almost allows herself a sigh of relief. The Needlemen! Hers to command! Let the Cat and Arthur Ness run where they may for now. The Queen's own hunters are about to be set loose. And from them, there is no escape.

"Your Grace is too kind," says Lady Eris. "I will not fail you."

"See that you do not," the Queen replies, her gaze boring deeper than ever into the place where Lady Eris' soul would be if she had one. "I am sure you are well aware of the dim view I take of failure."

Lady Eris' eyes glance again at the eyes and faces in the walls. The previous Noir Ladies. Lady Aerie, Lady Kray, Lady Taranteen and a dozen others. All defeated by the Cat. All of them now stitched by the Queen into the walls of her chambers. Unmoving, unblinking, yet still alive. Forever staring at the Queen they failed.

Lady Eris bows, low.

"My Queen – the Cat and Arthur Ness shall be yours in mere days. And our work in Waterwhistle shall be completed and you will have the final victory."

The Queen says nothing else. She simply produces another set of materials, silks, buttons, threads and sets to work on another doll to sit beside the one she has just finished. The doll of Arthur Ness.

Lady Eris leaves.

THE FIRST JOURNEY

Arthur stood on the deck of the *Galloping Snake* and stared, open mouthed at the black skies above him. The endless darkness enveloped them and crashed against the vast sphere of powerful, white fire that was the Arilon sun. The severe light sitting against the pure darkness had played havoc with Arthur's eyes at first but as they continued their journey away from Lady Eris' castle, his vision had eventually settled down. And soon, he had started to see the true beauty of the Arilon skies.

The overriding feature of their surroundings was, of course, the neverending dark. The purest, deepest black that Arthur had ever seen. This was surely what space looked like, he thought. It was exhilarating (even though the idea of being in space had always terrified him).

Dotted throughout the curtain of dark, though, were the stars - or what looked like stars. They were sprinkled across the skyscape like ever-so-sparse handfuls of fairy dust. Here and there, the stars were bunched together in odd little clusters.

The most visually striking thing though, hands-down, were the cables.

"What are they called again?" asked Arthur. "Travelling Lines?"

"Travel Lines," the Cat corrected. "They connect all the islands of Arilon together. Some islands have more, some have less. Ships are attached to them with an anchor chain that has a ring on the end and they just travel back and forth along the lines, through the NothingSpace."

Arthur marvelled at the sight of the Travel Lines in the darkness. Actually, it was more like he was marvelling at the *lack* of sight of them. The Lines themselves were all but invisible against the black of the sky. Only when you looked towards the sun could you see reflections of them as the sunlight lit them up. It was a bit like shining a torch in the darkness; you could see the floating dust particles but only the ones that passed near the light. You knew the rest of the air was just as full of dusty bits, you just couldn't see them.

Judging from the sheer amount of reflections that were illuminated near the sun, Arthur could tell the rest of the black space must be *filled* with Travel Lines. Clearly, the NothingSpace around them wasn't as empty as it seemed.

"Those points of light you can see," the Cat said, "aren't stars. They're intersections. Whenever the Travel Lines cross over or branch."

Arthur nodded. "Ah, I see, that's why they gather in bunches every so often – those are where the Travel Lines converge around the islands, aren't they?"

The Cat winked, impressed. "You're getting it, Arthur Arthur Ness."

"But, wait a minute…" Arthur was struck by a sudden thought. "There must be loads of ships out there right now, travelling along those lines. Maybe even the line we're on, coming towards us right now. What happens when two ships want to get past each other on the same Travel Line?"

"Simple. They crash into each other, explode and everyone dies."

Arthur stared at the Cat, agape. The Cat shrugged.

"Okay, note to self; don't joke about getting blown up. No, they simply rotate so one's above the Line and the other's below it. Then the anchor rings just pass through each other."

"Pass through…?"

"Well, not through like ghosts. I just mean they open and close in just the right way to let each other past while always keeping the ships connected to the Travel Line."

"That sounds complicated..." Arthur said, clearly unconvinced of the reliability of this arrangement. "And only very slightly more reassuring than the crashing, exploding thing."

The Cat smiled. "Don't worry, Arthur. The anchor rings are very advanced devices and crafted with the utmost care. After all, they're the most important thing in Arilon. Without them, ships wouldn't be able to hold onto the Travel Lines and nobody would be able to go anywhere."

"So... the ships don't actually fly, then?" Arthur asked.

The Cat laughed. "Now you're just being silly! Ships aren't the least bit aerodynamic, Arthur, I don't know if you never noticed. Making them fly unaided is kind of impossible."

Arthur looked up at the ship's sails. They were deep scarlet and black and full of wind, propelling the vessel along through the darkness. The strange thing was, though, that although the sails were clearly catching a gust, Arthur couldn't feel a thing. It was as though there was an impossible wind that only the sails could feel.

It was all so alien and crazy and exactly the kind of thing that should have sent him out of his mind with terror. Instead, Arthur was shocked to find himself suddenly laughing.

"This is all just *amazing!*" he shouted.

"Not too bad, is it? Bit different to Wotsitwhistle."

At the mention of the village, Arthur glanced around back up the deck to where Teresa stood at the ship's wheel, steering the ship to wherever it was they were going. He blushed a little as he remembered what a fool he'd made of himself when he'd come aboard. Stuttering and stammering like he'd met some famous movie star.

He'd tried to speak to her but he'd been so nervous, it had just come out as "heyoblahgle".

She'd laughed at his bumbling attempt at conversation, but not in an unkind way. Not like the bullies at school so often did. There was something about Teresa, Arthur felt. An easy friendliness as strange as it was comfortable. It felt to Arthur as though they'd been friends forever.

The Cat stood up and strode along the side-rails of the ship. He turned to Teresa and shouted out (much louder than a cat that small should have been able to, even a talking one), "Next left, I believe, Smithy!"

"Aye, aye, Cat!" she replied with a mock salute.

The Cat turned back to Arthur. "Best hold on for this bit."

Bemused, Arthur looked ahead. With no moving scenery, it was impossible to judge how fast they were going. But that suddenly changed when a Travel Line at right angles to the *Snake* suddenly appeared out of the darkness ahead and whipped toward them at breakneck speed. The cable lay right across their path, forming a junction. Where the two lines met, there was a tiny pinprick of light. The ship's anchor ring passed over the crossing of Travel Lines and a clacking noise rang out as it did its clever, superfast unclasping. The vessel swung round to the left almost like a toy being thrown around by a giant, playful hand. At the same time, there was a mighty **BUMP** which sent Arthur – who had forgotten to take the Cat's advice – sprawling to the floor.

The Cat laughed, long and loud. Arthur rubbed the back of his head but as he looked up, he saw a hand waiting to help him. He reached up and Teresa pulled him to his feet.

"Sorry about that." She grinned. "We just switched from one line to another. It's the only way you can change direction between islands. I'm gettin' the hang of it but I bet I'm not as good as the *Snake's* actual owner."

"So... the ship isn't yours?" asked Arthur.

"Ha! I wish!" Teresa straightened the black hair-band that kept her slightly chaotic, blonde mop out of her face. She turned to the Cat. "Is that the only Line Switch we have to make?"

The feline nodded. "Yep – we should arrive at Graft in about thirty minutes." He yawned. "Just enough time for me to catch a quick nap, I think."

And with that, the dropped down onto the deck and padded away. "Don't anybody go falling off the ship while I'm gone. See you in a bit, non-cats."

"Graft?" Arthur repeated to Teresa once the Cat had disappeared below decks.

"It's an island. You'll like it," she said. "The islands are *amazing*."

"Have you been to many?"

"One or two," Teresa said. "The Cat's told me about loads of 'em, though. I can't wait to see some more."

"You sound like you love it here."

Teresa grinned so wide, Arthur thought her face might split in two. "I've only been here a short while but... yeah, I really do! I've always wanted to travel," she said. "Get out, get on a boat, see the world. Didn't quite have *this* in mind, of course... Y'know, me dad always said..."

Immediately, upon mentioning her father, Teresa's smile faltered. Arthur realised that behind her fun and bravado, she'd been trying hard not to think of home.

"How... how is everyone?" she asked, eventually

"They're all okay... sort of..." Arthur tried to think of the least upsetting way of putting it. "I mean, they're not hurt or anything. They're under Lady Eris' control but they don't know anything's wrong. They're…"

"They've forgotten me, haven't they?" Teresa walked over to the side of the ship and gazed out into the nothingness.

"Everyone but Sam." Arthur came up behind her. "He's the one who told me about you."

"Sam's still okay?" Teresa jerked her gaze up to Arthur, hopefully. "And…what about me dad?"

Arthur was about to ask who her dad was until it suddenly came to him in a flash of realisation.

"Mr Smith! At the farm shop!" he exclaimed to himself as much as Teresa. "I went there every day for compost!"

Then he remembered what he had been buying the compost for and his smile faded.

"He's… he's the same as everyone else, I'm afraid," Arthur said, eventually.

Teresa nodded and her gaze went back out to the NothingSpace. Arthur knew what she was thinking. Her home, her friends, her family… everything she'd ever known was under the control of Lady Eris.

"The last time I saw everyone," she said, "I was standin' on a bench in the middle of the square. Tellin' everyone to throw Lady Eris out of town. I could see it in their eyes – I were reachin' 'em. But then the Yarnbulls grabbed me and everyone went back to bein' quiet. They stopped seein' me. Didn't even notice as I got dragged up the street, kickin' and screamin'."

"Where did the Yarnbulls take you?"

"To *her*," Teresa almost spat the word. "Lady Eris. She said I were causin' too much trouble and she were goin' to dispose of me. The Yarnbulls took me into the tapestry, into that castle and threw me in the dungeons."

"You were in actual dungeons?" Arthur was aghast. "All this time? On your own?"

"Oh, no," Teresa smiled a little, now. "Not on me own. There were some other Arilon folk in there. Told me where I was, what were goin' on. There were this one fella, Captain Thrace. Told me he'd figured out a way to escape and get to his ship, the *Gallopin' Snake*. Only problem was that you had to squeeze through a hole that were too small for everyone."

"Everyone except you," Arthur grinned. Teresa nodded. Her old energy and enthusiasm was back in her voice now as she recounted her thrilling tale.

"I got out, sneaked past the Yarnbulls and followed the Captain's instructions to where the *Snake* had been impounded by Lady Eris. He told me how to fly her so I sneaked on board and..." She laughed now as Arthur stared on, wide-eyed. "Don't ask me how, but I managed to fly her out of there. Right off the island before anyone could stop me!"

Arthur couldn't believe it. He tried to imagine how scared he would have been trying to sneak past Yarnbulls and steal an entire ship from under their noses. Safe to say, he wouldn't have even attempted it.

"Where did you go?" he asked.

"Well, Captain Thrace made me promise to find a way back in to get him and the others out," Teresa said. "So I flew the *Snake* around a bit – y'know, to get the hang of handling her – then I sneaked back down to the island. I tried to see if there were any way I could get into the dungeons. That's when I bumped into the Cat."

Arthur nodded. He knew what the Cat had been doing there. Spying on Lady Eris. And him.

"The Cat helped me out. Y'know, looked after me." Teresa continued. "We stayed on the *Snake*, just far enough away from the island to avoid bein' seen. And we popped down to the surface every so often to figure out how to rescue the Captain as well as for the Cat to keep visitin' you. He kept tellin' me about you, y'know. About how Lady Eris had you runnin' around in that house for her."

Arthur flushed with embarrassment. Why did Teresa have to know all about that? It wasn't his proudest moment or -

"I thought you must have been really brave," Teresa said, suddenly.

Arthur couldn't believe his ears. "Excuse me?"

Teresa nodded, unmistakable admiration on her face. "I couldn't have spent all that time with her in that spooky old house! But I thought, if you could stand to be around Lady Eris all the time, scary as she is, then I could find a way into those dungeons."

That's when Arthur realised what an odd situation they'd been in. They'd never met and yet not only had they heard of each other, they'd been each others' inspiration!

"So... did you find a way in?" he asked.

Teresa nodded. "I think so. But I didn't get a chance to try it out. I saw you and the Cat running out of the castle and I had to come and get you."

"Oh, yeah," Arthur said. "Sorry about that."

Teresa shrugged, a small grin on her face. "Not a problem. I'm sure the Cat will figure out a way for us to get back there and help Captain Thrace and the others."

The grin faltered for a second and Arthur knew why. They'd help the people in Lady Eris' dungeon but who was going to help the people back in Waterwhistle? Who was going to help her brother and her dad?

In that moment, Arthur realised what it was about Teresa that he liked. She was brave and brash and always full of grins. She could face down Yarnbulls and steal pirate ships all day long. And yet there was one thing she was afraid of – anything happening to her family or the people she cared about.

And Arthur suddenly felt that someone as brave and strong as Teresa deserved to have someone help her out when she needed it.

"We'll stop her," he said, suddenly, surprising himself with the strength in his voice. The tone wasn't lost on Teresa. Her eyes instantly jumped up to his. "I don't know how," Arthur went on, "but... we'll stop whatever it is Lady Eris is doing to Waterwhistle and we'll get everyone back to normal. I promise."

The words seemed to pick Teresa up straight away.

"You know what?" she said. "You're right. Who does she think she is, comin' into our village, spinnin' her spells. Doesn't she know we've got bigger things to worry about? There's a blummin' war on!"

They both laughed and Teresa was suddenly standing up straighter, back to her previous, worry-proof self.

"Hey, an' I'll tell you what else," she smirked, nudging Arthur on the shoulder. "I bet Lady Eris is right scared now that Arthur Ness is on the case!"

And even though she was joking, the way she said his name made Arthur feel ten feet tall.

THE BROKEN CROWN

Before Arthur actually saw the island of Graft, he saw its Travel Lines.

A cable became visible above them, parallel to the one they were on. Then another slightly further away. And then one below them and another to the left. The lines were all beginning to converge on the island, Arthur knew, even though the island itself was still hidden by the darkness. Already, Arthur could see it was going to be much, much bigger than the one they'd escaped from.

The Travel Lines began to appear in ever greater numbers. Arthur marvelled at how they popped into view and filled in the gaps between the already-visible points of light that joined them together. Like some cosmic dot to dot, Arthur thought with a grin.

Just a minute later, he saw his first ship. Some kind of passenger vessel, slightly smaller than the *Snake*. He could just about make out people on board getting their luggage together and preparing themselves for their imminent arrival on Graft. Then another cruiser, even smaller and rounder than the first came into view away to the left. Just as Arthur was beginning to think the *Galloping Snake* was the biggest ship around, though, he looked up and drew in a sharp breath of awe at the sight above him. The massive, hulking underside of another ship passing overhead. He didn't know if it was another cruiser or a merchant trader or something else… but whatever it was, it dwarfed the *Snake*.

There were scores, of ships now, Arthur saw. All looming out of the darkness one by one. Craft of all shapes and sizes moved up and down the lines, switching from one to another via the junction points, illuminated by a hundred tiny points of light.

At first, the lines had all been pointing towards the presence of something unseen, hovering in the Black just beyond the grasp of eager eyes. But soon, an unbelievably huge shape lumbered out of the darkness.

Arthur held his breath in sheer wonder at the sight before him. It was basically a floating horizon, cut away from its surrounding world and placed, hanging, in space. The bottom half was completely flat while the top face was covered in buildings and people, hills and valleys, fields and forests. It was like an infeasibly huge plate crammed with life and shapes and movement ontop and nothing underneath.

Lady Eris' island had been absolutely *tiny* in comparison to this.

"Welcome to Graft," said the Cat, wandering up behind Arthur. "It's a cosy little place, nice and out of the way."

"Little?" Arthur scoffed. "It's massive!"

"There are lots of bigger islands in Arilon," said the Cat. "You'll be seeing them soon, no doubt. But this one's a good place to start."

Even from as far out as they were, it took another half hour or more to finally reach the surface. By the time they got close, darkness was falling over the island and Arthur noticed the sun was in a different relative position than it had been earlier. He stifled a laugh of wonder as he realised the island was actually *rotating*.

Teresa guided the *Galloping Snake* towards what looked to Arthur like the island's main ship port. There were dozens of wooden platforms sticking out from the main dock. Most of them had vessels of various sizes docked there. Teresa picked an empty bay and followed the Travel Line down to it.

Slowly and smoothly, Teresa eased the galleon towards the wooden gantry that waited for them. They finally came to a stop between two huge cargo boats. They were bigger than the *Snake*, Arthur saw. (Though, to him, nowhere near as cool).

As the trio walked down the ship's gangplank and onto the quayside, the hustle and bustle of Graft was beginning to fill Arthur's senses. This was more like London, he thought. Lots of people, lots of noise, lots of smells. Yes, he thought, a great smile on his face, he could definitely get used to this place.

The place looked old-fashioned to Arthur. Almost medieval or something like that. Horse and cart seemed to be the main method of transport. People dressed in simple, roughspun clothes and a few had swords (actual swords!) hanging from their belts. The crowds clamoured on all sides and voices shouted a thousand thousand things. There were smells of food being cooked and sold at the roadside and above them, the streetlights were blinking on one at a time as the nighttime darkness descended. Considering the places didn't appear to have electricity, Arthur wondered just what was powering the lamps.

As alien as it all seemed, it also seemed completely normal. There were farmers, miners, labourers… they could have been taken straight from the towns and cities back home, Arthur thought. The buildings that surrounded them were factories, warehouses and all kinds of places of work. People were streaming out of them with expressions of weariness and happiness – the satisfaction of hard work well done.

"Here on Graft," said Teresa as they pushed through the crowded street, "everyone works hard. The adults work hard at various jobs and the kids work hard at school.When they finish school, they do their homework then they go out to their night-time jobs and they work hard at those, too."

"Sounds like a tough life," said Arthur.

"Indeed it is," the Cat said, leaping up onto Arthur's shoulders. "Oh, you don't mind do you? Lots of feet down there. Anyway, yes, the people of Graft *do* have a bit of a tough life. Which is why, when they've finished their night-jobs, many kids head to places like the one we're going to now."

"Which is where, exactly?" Arthur asked.

Teresa smiled. "The pub."

Arthur waggled a finger in his ear, pretending to clean it out. "I'm sorry, I don't think I heard you properly. It sounded like you said we were going to a pub."

"It's called the Broken Crown," said the Cat.

Arthur's mouth dropped open. "You... you're serious, we're going to a pub?"

"Oh, don't worry," laughed the Cat. "They don't serve alcohol at kids' pubs. But they do have over fifty kinds of pop and more types of juice than you can shake a Yarnbull horn at."

Arthur shook his head. A pub for kids..! He seriously didn't think there was anything else that could surprise him, now.

"Hey, where's my bone?" came a deep voice from behind Arthur. "Where's my bone? Anyone seen my bone?"

He turned round just in time to see a big, hulking dog trotting up the road, nose to the ground. "Where's that blummin' bone got to?" the dog muttered to himself.

A horse, tied up outside a shop, shook its long head as it watched the frantic hound scuttle past and huffed, "Stupid dog."

The Cat roared with laughter when he saw Arthur's face.

"What," he laughed, "you thought I was the only talking animal? We're not all as stupid as the creatures in your world, you know!"

Before long, the trio arrived at a ramshackle building in the centre of town. A wooden sign hung high over the door, swinging softly in the gentle night breeze. And on the sign, the name 'The Broken Crown' with the picture of a crown in two pieces, the gems and jewels, scattered over a rough, wooden tabletop.

The building didn't seem to be in much better state than the crown, Arthur thought. Some of the paint was peeling and one of the window shutters was hanging off. And yet, despite all that, the place seemed to give off an odd sense of comfort and friendliness – probably down to the windows that glowed a warm orange from all the activity inside.

As they headed through the door, Arthur was glad to see his instincts had been correct. The place was absolutely crammed wall-to-wall with kids of all ages. But rather than the rowdy noise he'd heard when going past pubs in

London, this place felt like a collection of friends relaxing and swapping stories about a long day.

The Cat directed them towards the bar and they pushed through the throng of people. Standing behind the counter, serving a neverending sea of customers was a big, round man with a bushy moustache and a very grumpy-looking face. He was dishing out drinks while a skinny, young fellow wandered around with a tray, collecting empty cups and glasses.

"Frogham!" the Cat shouted and the big barman looked up at them. Straight away, the sour expression melted away and the big man was suddenly all smiles.

"Cat!" Frogham called back. "You're alive! I'd heard the Queen had stuffed you and mounted you on her mantelpiece!"

"Well, it wasn't a mantelpiece," said the Cat, "more like a trinket shelf. Ah, but wait 'til you hear how I escaped…"

"A-HEM!" Teresa cleared her throat very loudly and both old friends stopped in mid-sentence, staring at her.

"Oh, I'm sorry," she said, sarcastically. "Did me dyin' of thirst interrupt your conversation?"

Frogham laughed a laugh so loud and deep, Arthur could feel it in his shoes.

"Hey, Cat, I like this one!" the barman nodded at Teresa. "Where'd you find 'er?"

"Well, we have a lot of catching up to do so why don't you set us up with something to eat and drink and a nice, private table at the back…" said the Cat, "…and I'll tell you all about it."

BLASTBERRIES
AND CATCHING UP

It wasn't until Arthur started his meal that he realised how ravenously hungry he was. It turned out daring escapes made for hungry work. But as tasty as the meat and potato stew had been, the highlight of the meal was definitely his drink. A tall, cold glass of something called blastberry juice.

"This is delicious!" he said for the sixth time, wiping the sweet, sticky stuff from round his mouth with the back of his hand. He set the glass of juice down and stared again at the swirling orange and crimson lights dancing about inside. "I've never heard of a blastberry before."

"They only grow in Arilon," the Cat said, lapping up his fizzy milk. "You have to pick them wearing metal gloves. In case they explode."

"Ex...explode..?" Arthur looked up.

"Oh, yes," the Cat went on. "Squeeze a ripe blastberry too hard, it could take your whole hand off." He looked up from his milk and smiled at Arthur. "But they're scrummy, yes?"

"Don't worry," Teresa smirked at Arthur's worried face. "Once they've been picked, they're safe. No more boom boom."

"Unless you shake it really hard," said the Cat. "Fizz it right up. People dancing with unopened tins of blastberry juice in their pockets tend to get very nasty surprises. Puts a severe crimp in your foxtrot."

Somewhat nervously, Arthur took another sip of the juice. He fancied he could almost feel tiny explosions as it slid down his throat and into his stomach. But, he thought with a grin, it was that slightly dangerous stinging that just made it all the tastier.

"But…" the Cat said as he finally finished the last of his drink, "…we didn't escape from crazed cow monsters just to talk about blastberries, did we?"

Arthur suddenly realised this was the part he'd been dreading. Flying around on borrowed pirate ships was fun. Lady Eris and Yarnbulls and whatever was happening to Waterwhistle was *not* fun. Arthur had a horrible feeling that the next few minutes were going to make him aware of just how much danger he was really in.

And then they'll know what kind of a scaredy-cat you really are, won't they?

Frogham came bustling over, another tray of drinks in his meaty hands.

"These ones are on the house as well," said the barman, "on account a'your miraculous return from the dead, me feline friend!"

His face was so jolly now, it was hard for Arthur to imagine the grumpy-looking man they'd seen before.

"Right, let's get down to it, then," the barman said as he took a seat at the table. "Young Stick'll keep the punters 'appy for a spell but e' ain't too bright, bless 'im. 'Fore long, he'll ferget to ask the customers for any money, like as not."

Arthur peeked up from his stew and looked Frogham up and down, as much as he dared. He was friendly enough but this was a new person into the small circle. The Cat seemed to notice Arthur's apprehension.

"What we're about to discuss, Arthur," the Cat said, "you'll see there's a conflict going on. And there are sides. And Frogham here, he's on ours."

"Good blummin' thing, too," the barman said, "takin' wanted fugitives under me roof."

Arthur gulped. He knew it. Wanted fugitives.

"Okay, are you sitting comfortably?" the Cat asked, pulling his second bowl of fizzy milk toward him. Arthur nodded, gingerly. He could see Teresa glancing around the pub rather than preparing to listen to the Cat – clearly, she'd already had this talk.

"Right then," the Cat said to Arthur. "Let's start with the islands…"

- THE IDEA ISLANDS -

"You see," he started, "everyone on Arilon lives on the islands. But they're not just pieces of land like in your world. Each island is an Idea. Let's take where we are now. Graft. You see, Graft's Idea is 'hard work'. The people here know the value of putting in a solid day's work and getting the satisfaction of a job well done in return.

"You saw when we arrived that this island has lots of Travel Lines. Well, it's not just the ships that use them. Ideas travel along them, too. Those Lines out there transmit Graft's Idea out to the rest of Arilon. Through them, people all over Arilon feel the Idea of hard work.

"Popular Ideas come from islands with lots of Lines. Hard work. Fun. Greed. And then, there are those Ideas that only a few people feel strongly. Charity. Murder. Bravery…"

"Okay…" said Arthur, "…so some islands have more control over people's thoughts than others, I get it. But… what does all that have to do with the Queen?"

"Well…" said the Cat, looking down into his milk, "…that's where it starts to get rather unfortunate…"

- THE QUEEN -

"The Queen ain't actually a Queen," said Frogham, taking over. "She just showed up, one day and *declared* 'erself Queen."

"Didn't you fight her?" Arthur asked.

"With what?" the barman shrugged. "Arilon ain't got no army. Jus' peacekeepers – and they ain't really set up to deal with that kind a' conflict. See, what you got to understand, Arthur, is that, naturally, Arilon's in a state a' *balance*."

Arthur was confused, "Balance…?"

The Cat moved the salt and pepper shakers so they stood a few inches apart. Then, he pressed a paw down on the curved end of a fork so the handle rose up. Arthur picked up the fork and, seeing what the Cat wanted him to do, rested it carefully across the top of the two shakers, forming a bridge.

The Cat went on. "It's all in the way the islands are connected. There are bad Ideas – like greed or jealousy. But good Ideas, too. Kindness, helpfulness and so on. We feel them all but there are more connections to the good Ideas than the bad ones.

"Yes, some people are more naturally bad than others so they feel the nasty Ideas more strongly, even though there are less connections to them. Those people sometimes do nasty things, so we have the peacekeepers to keep them in check. But, generally, most people are good most of the time."

Arthur nodded in understanding, looking down at the fork bridge. "I see. Balance."

"The Queen changed all that, though," said Frogham, shaking his head. "See, Arthur, she decided that she wanted to control everyone in Arilon. That meant controlling what they think an' feel. So…"

Arthur suddenly saw where this was going. "She started cutting the Travel Lines, didn't she?"

The Cat smiled, impressed.

"That, she did, boy, that she did," Frogham looked sad, all of a sudden. Sad and tired. "She travels around Arilon with 'er fleet of warships, trimmin' and prunin' the Travel Lines. Like she's growin' a plant that she wants to shape just so.

"One a' the first islands she went to was Duseeya. Their Idea is Self-Reliance. They know – so we all know – that if you rely on yerself rather than waitin' for everyone else to do everythin' for yer, then you're in more control of yer life.

"The Queen cut hundreds a' cables from that island. There's only a few left, now. The Idea of Self-Reliance suddenly got a lot weaker right across Arilon."

Arthur nodded. "Well, that must help the Queen," he said. "Nobody thinks its their responsibility to fight her. Everyone waits for someone else to do it. That means *nobody* does it."

"She's messin' with the way people feel," said Frogham, "which messes with the way they *think*. Which messes with the way they *act*."

The Cat knocked the salt shaker over and the fork clattered to the table. Arthur nodded.

No more balance.

"But… but what about you lot?" Arthur asked. "You're still fighting her."

"People are still individuals," said the Cat. "They're still clever or selfish or kind or greedy. Depending on how much of those you naturally feel, you'll feel certain Ideas more or less."

"So, if you're a naturally brave person," asked Arthur, "and the Queen cuts Travel Lines to the Bravery island, then you'll be less brave, but still more brave than others..?"

The Cat grinned. "Precisely. Naturally brave, that's us."

"Yeah…" Frogham took a drink. "Or naturally stupid."

"So…" Arthur mulled the information over in his mind, "…the Queen wants to control all of Arilon. But why? If she already owns an armada and stuff, she must already be rich."

"It's not money that drives the Queen," said the Cat, "It's power. She wants to control everyone just to control them. She has no other purpose, no other desire. She just wants to hold everyone in her hands as if we were nothing but dolls…"

The Cat was staring into the half-distance now, recalling something in his mind as he talked about the

Queen. Some memory or knowledge, Arthur thought, that he wasn't sharing with the rest of them.

Another question popped into Arthur's head.

"What about us?" Arthur said. "Me and Teresa? Does it work on humans, too, this cable-cutting thing?"

"Not really," said the Cat, his attention coming back to his surroundings. "Human minds are very similar to ours but you're not plugged into our islands. You seem quite resistant to the Ideas – more likely to stick to your own."

"Do you get many humans in Arilon?" Arthur asked.

"Not many," Frogham said. "But every so often, some humans do fall through to this world, one way or another."

Arthur definitely wanted to hear more about that but thought perhaps now wasn't the time to ask.

"Judging from the activity in Waterwhistle," the Cat went on, "it looks like those travellers have given old Queenie the idea of going on some trips of her own. Looks like she wants to head out into the Human World. And once she gets there, I think it's safe to say she'll set about doing the same thing there as she's doing here."

"But, how..?" Arthur asked. "Our ideas aren't connected together by cables."

The Cat looked as though he was about to say something – but, in the end, whatever it was, he decided to leave for another time.

"The only thing we know," he shrugged, eventually, "is that Lady Eris is Binding the inhabitants of Waterwhistle so she can take their thoughts into her direct control."

"But, why?" asked Arthur.

"I don't know," admitted the Cat as he lapped up the last of his fizzy milk. "That's why we're going to ask Bamboo."

Frogham raised his bushy eyebrows in surprise. "You're goin' ter see Bamboo? You think you'll be able ter find 'im? You know how hard 'e is ter track down!"

"Plus, you told me he were crazier than a sack of cuckoo birds," said Teresa.

"Okay, okay," said the Cat. "Yes, he can be hard to find. And yes, he is a little on the eccentric side. But he's pretty much the best Weaver in the whole of Arilon. Probably even better than the Queen. He should be able to give us some insight into what's going on in Waterwhistle."

Frogham nodded in approval. "Well, speakin' of which, could you ask 'im a couple of questions about me pub? Me packet snacks aren't sellin', see, and I wondered if..." and with that Frogham and the Cat wandered off into the crowded tavern, chatting away, leaving Arthur and Teresa behind like an afterthought.

"Bye, then!" Teresa waved to them, sarcastically. She turned to Arthur and rolled her eyes, smiling. "Sometimes it's better to just leave him to it, I reckon. The Cat knows what he's doin'."

Arthur nodded. Weavers? Bamboo? Islands? Ideas? The confusion on Arthur's face didn't go unnoticed by Teresa.

"Lot to get your head around, isn't there?" she said.

"It all makes sense," Arthur said, "it's just a bit... new."

"I felt exactly the same way when the Cat told me." Teresa nudged Arthur's shoulder and grinned. "Don't worry. I'll look after you. You'll be alright."

Arthur smiled. Teresa did have a knack of making him feel better but it didn't hide the fact that, bit by bit, he was beginning to feel way out of his depth.

Arthur liked the Cat but he did seem a little too reckless and carefree. As though this was all just a game to him. He'd seen Arthur being bossed about by Lady Eris and decided to recruit him into this little war – but what if Arthur hadn't wanted to join? Lady Eris had tried to control Arthur. If the Cat was trying to make Arthur do things he didn't want to do, then how was that any different?

All kinds of confusing thoughts bumped and bashed around inside Arthur's head. Rather than saying anything, though, and making himself look stupid, he kept quiet and finished his blastberry juice.

There was a jingling and clattering of glasses, suddenly, and Stick – Frogham's barboy – came stumbling up to the table.

"Um… any a' yoo seen Mr. Frogham? I thinks we done run out of Stink Juice. Ain't no more comin' out the taps."

Teresa pointed into the crowd. "He went that way, somewhere, with the Cat."

Stick fumbled with the tray of glasses, nearly dropping it. "Oh gosh, okay. Cuz the Stink Juice… it's so popular… people's gettin' all uppity about it…" but by now, he was wandering off, talking to himself, the two children completely forgotten.

Teresa and Arthur looked at each other – and burst out laughing.

"Come on," Teresa wiped the tears of laughter from her eyes, "don't tell me you don't love this place!"

"Well," admitted Arthur, "it's certainly growing on me."

The Cat suddenly popped up onto the table from nowhere.

"Honestly, leave you two alone for five seconds and you start giggling. It's like you're children or something," he said. "Now buckle down. We've got work to do."

"Before you start going on about this Bamboo fella again," Teresa said, "can I remind you I've got a promise to keep?"

The Cat nodded. "Don't worry, I hadn't forgotten. I'm already planning how to rescue Captain Thrace from Eris' dungeons. We owe him. Without him getting you out of there, Teresa, we wouldn't be sat here now." Then the Cat smirked, "Besides, breaking people out of Lady Eris' personal dungeons will annoy her no end. And annoying Lady Eris is like the dot on my 'i'. The shine on my shoes. The cherry on my cream cake…"

Again, Arthur noted how much fun the Cat was having in the face of serious danger.

"Okay," said the Cat. "Let's eat some Orange Rocket Cake, warm up our best action music and figure out how to break *into* a prison!"

SHUTTING UP SHOP
(from the initially happy thoughts of Karl Frogham)

It was good ter see the Cat again. So glad he ain't dead. It'd make fighting the Queen kinda difficult if he was. He's the only thing she's scared of. Heavens, if I knows why.

"You need anything else before I go, Mr. Frogham?" asks Stick.

"I just need yer to go and fetch them barrels of Mudwater in from the back," I say. "Then you can get off 'ome."

"Right you are, Mr. Frogham," says Stick and he disappears out the back door.

I like Stick - hard worker, very polite. Thicker than a plank a' wood, mind, but I s'pose you can't have everythin'.

The front door creaks open and three men walk in. Tall, thin. Look like undertakers. They're wearin' identical black suits which is immediately suspicious since there ain't many folk on Graft that wear suits, not ones this expensive lookin'. They got pristine, white shirts and perfectly straight black ties. And then they got wide-brimmed hats what cover most of their faces. All's I can see are their noses and thin, cruel-lookin' mouths. Their hands are all in their pockets except the one at the front who's carryin' a small, black, leather valise. His bony, white fingers are clutchin' the bag handle like 'is life depends on it. The weirdest thing is they all look exactly the same. Like triplets or somethin'.

"Take us to the cat," the middle one says.

I shrug me shoulders and keep wipin' the bar top down. "What cat?"

"The talking cat," says the one on the left.

"The one with no name," says the one on the right.

"There's lots a' talking cats frequents this establishment," I say, tryin' to hide how nervous I am. "Talkin' dogs, too. Whether or not they 'ave names ain't no business a' mine."

"So you will not tell us where the cat and the human boy are?" the one on the left asks again.

I go cold. They know about Arthur. But I keep on wipin' the bar top and shrug.

"Very well," says the middle stranger.

He puts the black bag down on my countertop and I can finally see his hands properly. Me grip tightens on the cloth in shock when I see his fingers. 'Cause they ain't really fingers at all. They're long, thin, sharp, shiny lengths of metal. Straight away, I know what these strangers are.

Needlemen.

People talk about 'em in hushed, scared voices. They're the stuff of late-night stories and myths. Sometimes, children are told that if they're naughty, the Needlemen will come and get 'em. But no-one believes they're actually real 'cause no-one's ever seen one.

Well... no-one that's lived to tell the tale.

The Needleman clicks open the valise and reaches inside. He takes out a small, rolled up piece a' cloth which he then lays on the bar top I just finished wipin'.

"If you will not co-operate..." says the one on the left.

"...you will be replaced," says the one on the right.

The middle one unrolls the cloth. It looks like a small table mat except it's got all these tiny pictures of faces on it. But the faces are all blank. No eyes, no mouths or noses. Except one. One of the faces is filled in. And I recognise it. Blessed islands, I recognise it!

But it's too late for me to warn anyone what I've discovered - the Needleman's fingers 'ave started moving. He waves 'em over the mat, super-speed, like he's typin' some infernal words onto an invisible typewriter. The needle-fingers are glistenin' in the dim light of the wall-torches as they burn low. They're shinin' as they start to move so fast, they all just become one big, shimmerin' blur.

I look into the mat again and I can feel it tuggin' me. I feel terrified of something, but I don't know what. Suddenly, threads shoot out of the mat, wrappin' around me. As they wrap around me, I can see them wrappin' around the stranger, too. But as they cover me up, they change him. Change him to look like *me!*

He smiles at me with my face.

Then I fall towards the mat, towards one of the blank faces and everythin' goes bl-

BARRELS DONE
(from the simple thoughts of Mikkal 'Stick' Stikkelson)

I pokes me head into the pub. I thoughts I heard some commotion. Shouting or somesuch. But Mr. Frogham's standing behind the bar, wiping the top down and whistling. Hmph. Must've 'magined it. Always 'maginin' things, me. Mr. Frogham says I should do less 'maginin' and more workin'.

"I'm all done, Mr. Frogham," I say.

He waves to me. "Okay, I'll see yer tomorrow. Tell yer old mother I said 'ello."

I nod. "Yessir, I will."

"Oh, and tell 'er not to worry about 'er back. I'm sure it'll get better with rest."

I frown. "How did you knows about that? I didn't think I'd mentioned it..."

Mr. Frogham looks at me and smiles. It's a strange smile. Kind of looks like he's using his face for the first time, getting' used to how it works.

"Didn't you know, Stick?" he says. "I'm very good at findin' things out. Give me enough time... I'll know *everythin'*."

CREEPING FEAR

Arthur stood alone on the deck of the *Galloping Snake* and stared at the Travel Line as it stretched away into the darkness. Although he couldn't see it, he knew exactly what waited on the other end of that Line. He knew exactly what it looked like and he knew just how terrified he was of seeing it again.

But, for their plan to work, he was going to have to go to Lady Eris' castle once again.

The burst of bravery he'd felt that led him to steal the mirror from Lady Eris' safe felt like a million years ago, now. And it had largely evaporated by the time he'd jumped through the tapestry with the Cat. By then, he was just running for his life.

The wonder of experiencing Arilon had been so awe-inspiring, he'd forgotten to be scared for a while. But now they were back in the thick of things. Going toe-to-toe with Lady Eris.

Welcome back, fear.

Welcome back? I never left.

Arthur put his hand into his shorts pocket and felt the tin of blastberry juice. He'd put it there for safekeeping, but it was making him nervous, sitting there. He took it out and placed it carefully on the siderails on the edge of the ship (the gunwhales, Teresa had told him they were called – he was going to have to remember the proper names for the parts of the ship).

Leaving the bright green tin standing there against the blackness of the NothingSpace, Arthur reached over to the telescope. Time to check again.

The shiny, brass scope was fixed to the gunwhale and Arthur swivelled it so it was pointing along the Travel Line and he put his eye to the end.

Although Lady Eris' castle was still too far away for the naked eye to see, the telescope somehow punched through the darkness with ease. Just as it had done the first six times he'd looked, Arthur's stomach lurched a little as the dark grey castle came into view. Touching the cold metal, Arthur inched the telescope down a bit, past the castle ramparts and main gate. Then along a bit, off to the side, beyond the courtyard.

No-one was there. Yet.

He moved away from the telescope and took a deep breath. On the one hand, he was glad. He didn't have to make his move yet. On the other hand, it just meant that the moment was still to come. Waiting for something scary to happen was even worse than the scary thing itself, Arthur thought.

The slight swaying motion of the *Galloping Snake* reminded Arthur of the only time, before coming to Arilon, that he'd ever been on a boat.

"Dad! Look!" Arthur pointed into the sky as he held tight to the edge of the small rowboat.

Arthur's father looked up in time to see a formation of four spitfires go speeding by overhead. Arthur grinned from ear to ear. The droning hum was deafening but extremely thrilling. The planes held a tight diamond shape as they passed.

"What formation is that, dad?" Arthur asked.

Arthur's father smiled. "We call that the 'show off to the people on the ground' formation."

As the planes disappeared into the distance – large, black shapes slowly turning into tiny, black dots – the hum softened to a distant buzz and the tranquil silence of the lake returned.

The fishing trip went back to being just Arthur and his dad. He knew why they'd come. His dad was going back to the base tomorrow. He was flying off to fight Hitler. This was going to be their last time alone together.

"When you're up there," Arthur asked, "being shot at... isn't it frightening?"

"Well, you're not up there alone," his father said. "You're in a squadron. Your mates are up there with you. And when the enemy are shooting and your mates need your help... well, there's no *time* to get scared."

Arthur checked the telescope. Again, nothing.

But wait-

Specks, at first. Then, very quickly, the specks became figures. Teresa. The Cat. Some other people.

And Yarnbulls.

Arthur grabbed the tin of blastberry juice and stuffed it back into his short pockets. He ran over to the ship's wheel and span it round. At the same time, he threw the large, wooden lever forward just as Teresa showed him. Instantly, suddenly, the sails filled with the mysterious, unfelt wind and the *Galloping Snake* lurched off towards Lady Eris' castle.

No time to be scared?

Arthur hoped his father was right.

RETURN TO CASTLE ERIS

Almost immediately, the island and the castle emerged out of the darkness. The fear flooded through Arthur's veins with full force as he saw with his own eyes the turrets, the walls, the gates of Castle Eris.

And yet, his grip tightened even more onto the ship's wheel and through gritted teeth, Arthur whispered;

"*Faster... faster...*"

The *Snake* picked up more and more speed as it arrowed down towards the island. The ship's anchor ring whipped along the Travel Line, making a strong, droning **thrummmm** that got louder as the ship picked up more speed.

Arthur could see the others with his naked eyes now. Teresa and the Cat were hurtling as fast as they could towards the island edge, followed by a straggley bunch of strangers (no doubt, the prisoners) and chased by a horde of enraged Yarnbulls.

The strange menagerie of characters was getting nearer and nearer to the island's edge. Any moment now, the Yarnbulls would have them trapped.

Suddenly, the moment was right and Arthur yelled to himself;

"*Now!*"

He pulled the motion lever all the way back and the huge sails fell away to nothing, the mysterious wind, dismissed. But the ship still had loads of momentum – it was slowing down a little but it was still hurtling toward the ground.

And that was where the next stage of the plan came in.

Arthur grabbed the wheel and spun it to the right as hard and fast as he could. Hand over hand, faster, faster. And slowly, the big ship started to turn. Still following the Travel Line, the *Snake* was turning slowly to the right, coming down sideways – almost *skidding* like Arthur used to do on his bike down the Commons road.

For just a second, Arthur imagined what he must look like. A young boy, just ten years old, steering a pirate ship all alone. Speeding into danger. Moments away from being smashed to pieces on the shore of an island. And for just a second, just the slightest moment, did he feel just the slightest touch of...

...excitement?

But then the moment was over as he saw the ground coming up towards him way too fast.

"Come on, come *on!*" Arthur span the wheel until it couldn't move anymore and then he held it in place, the ship fully turned to its side, now, skidding, sliding towards the island's surface and Arthur willed it and willed it and willed it to slow down but the ground was coming too, too fast and Arthur was going to crash and destroy the ship and kill himself and his friends and the prisoners.

"*Stop*, you stupid ship! *STOP!*"

And the *Galloping Snake* bumped gently onto the ground.

Arthur blinked.

A perfect landing!

"Arthur!" came the Cat's voice from somewhere down below. "The ladder!"

Oh. Yes. Right. Rescue in progress.

He ran back over to the side of the ship and unhooked the three rope ladders that were attached to the side. He threw the ends down and they unrolled open, one after the other. The Cat, Teresa and the prisoners all immediately began to scramble up them.

Arthur looked up into the courtyard. The familiar howl of enraged Yarnbulls reminded him that danger was still hot on the Cat's heels.

Time for his next task.

He took the blastberry juice out of his pocket and shook it. Really, really hard.

Arthur could feel the tin begin to vibrate, as though it were filled with rocks, all bashing against each other, fighting to get out. The tin started to jump in his hand. It took all Arthur's strength to keep it from dropping out onto the deck. Arthur grabbed the struggling tin with both hands and held it over the flaming torch next to the telescope.

Very suddenly, the tin got hot. Very hot. And even more jumpy. With a final effort, Arthur threw the blastberry juice as far and hard as he could in the direction of the Yarnbulls.

The creatures had almost reached the *Snake's* hull – just moments away from grabbing the final prisoners as they leapt onto the hanging ladders. Arthur knew his throw would be rubbish. At school, the PE teachers had virtually banned him from cricket. Even before the tin of juice had gone far, Arthur knew his failure was imminent.

"You need to make sure you get a direct hit on the Yarnbulls," the Cat said. In the background, Teresa prepared to leave the ship and head down to the Castle to free the prisoners.

Arthur looked at the juice tin in his hands. "This little tin's going to make the Yarnbulls retreat?" he asked.

"The Yarnbulls are made of yarn…" the Cat began.

Arthur's eyes widened. "Really?"

"You really are a dimwit, aren't you, Arthur Arthur Ness?" the Cat rolled his eyes. "Yes, they're made of actual yarn. And yarn is extremely flammable. One little spark and it all goes up in flames. The Yarnbulls aren't afraid of much… but they're *very* scared of fire."

"And… what if I miss?"

The Cat cocked an eyebrow. "Then you get this ship all to yourself."

BOOM!

The tin exploded directly over the Yarnbulls – exactly where Arthur had been told to put it. He punched the air in celebration as flaming blobs of molten blastberry juice cascaded down over the creatures in streaks of crimson and orange. And just as the Cat predicted, the Yarnbulls shrieked in terror and ran away as fast as they could. Tiny globules of molten berry had fallen on one or two of the beasts and sprouted into licks of flame.

"Wake up, Arthur!" the Cat cried, suddenly up on the gunwhale at Arthur's elbow. Behind him, Teresa and the prisoners were scrambling over the side and dropping onto the deck.

"I mean, we can hang around if you like," said the Cat. "Maybe Lady Eris will hear about us being here and come through from Waterwhistle with tea and chocolates."

At the mention of Lady Eris' name, Arthur jolted his eyes away from the Yarnbulls.

"Right," Arthur said to himself, under his breath. He sprinted up to the bridge and threw the motion lever forward once more. Instantly the sails billowed up again and the ship lurched forward. Arthur span the wheel hard to the right and the *Galloping Snake* lifted up, swinging, turning away from the island. Pointing back towards the welcoming black of the NothingSpace, Arthur pushed the lever full forward and the ship sped up, up and away at full tilt.

Within moments – and for the second time in two days – Lady Eris' island disappeared into the Black behind them and was gone.

"Well done, Arthur," the Cat said, unmistakable pride in his voice. "You did it!"

Arthur held onto the ship's wheel, out of breath, scared and jelly-kneed and he realised the Cat was right.

He blumming-well *had*.

CAPTAIN CHADWELL THRACE

If Arthur had to be honest, the old man in front of him didn't look much like a pirate captain.

He was unshaven, his scraggly white hair was unkempt and wild. He wore a long, dirty overcoat, draped limply over an old tunic and britches And to top it all off, he had two good eyes – not an eyepatch in sight.

Okay, Arthur had to admit, he *had* been locked up in Lady Eris' dungeons for months. But still… he was more Scruff-beard than Blackbeard. Disappointing.

Arthur was shaken from his thoughts by the last of the prisoners as they left the ship.

"Bye, Arthur," the round, middle-aged man (who smelt more than a little of rat droppings) shook Arthur's hand vigourously as he left the ship. "Fantastic flying! Just jiggetty!"

"Jiggetty?" the Cat cocked an eyebrow. "What the heck does *that* mean?"

Teresa shrugged, "It means 'brilliant', I suppose…"

The Cat shook his head, "You non-cats and your nonsense words…"

And with a final wave to Teresa and the Cat, the last ex-prisoner hobbled down the gangplank, onto the bustling docks of the island called Exeo and vanished into the crowd. Arthur looked out over the place, trying to figure out what it was about this place that had been bugging him since they'd arrived. Then he suddenly realised what it was – none of the buildings had any windows. Not a single one.

"Well, then…" came a voice, suddenly in Arthur's ear.

Arthur jumped as a hand landed on his shoulder and he turned to see the tall figure of Captain Thrace standing over him. Arthur gulped. The old man seemed a lot more fearsome close up.

"I have to thank ye, Arthur Ness. That were some mighty fine flyin', 'tis true. Mighty fine."

Arthur nodded, words stuck in his throat. Thrace turned to the Cat.

"And to you, creature, for mastermindin' the operation."

"It's not 'creature', it's 'Cat'," said the small feline. "With a capital 'C'."

Thrace nodded and touched his cap in apology. Then he turned to Teresa and smiled for the first time.

"And to you, girlie, for comin' back for me just like ye promised, I owe a special treasure-chest-full a' gratitude." And he bowed, making Teresa blush a little.

Then he stood up, "Okay. Now all a' yer, get the hell off me ship."

The Cat blinked, puzzled. "I'm sorry – is that some kind of pirate joke? Because if it is, I don't get it."

The old captain kicked open a wooden panel by his feet, pulled something out of it and spun round – and all of a sudden, he was pointing a very dangerous-looking pistol at the Cat and his companions.

"Well, if ye didn't get the last joke," said the Captain, "then ye certainly won't be laughin' at *this* one. Off. Now."

And just five minutes later, the Cat, Teresa and Arthur all stood on the docks of Exeo watching the

Galloping Snake disappear along a Travel Line and get swallowed up into the black.

"Well..." said the Cat, "...isn't that just jiggetty."

CAPTAIN CHADWELL THRACE ...AGAIN

The cat and the two human children stood on the docks, amid tugboats and liners and transport boats and they looked up into the black sky, utterly dumbfounded.

"He... he left us!" Arthur finally found his voice.

"It's fine," said the Cat.

And Teresa said, "That low down, dirty, double-crossin', backstabbin', stinky-faced, lice-ridden, scruffy-lookin' *nerf herder!*"

"It's fine," said the Cat.

"What's a nerf?" Arthur asked. Teresa spat on the ground.

"I don't know, but whatever it is, it's as low down, stinky-faced and lice ridden as *him!*" She shouted the last word up into the black Exeo sky.

"It's fine," said the Cat.

"Why do you keep sayin' it's fine?" Teresa shouted at the Cat. But the Cat, his eyes never leaving the sky, just smiled. The two children looked where he was looking.

And as they watched, the *Galloping Snake* suddenly emerged from the darkness and came sliding down towards them.

"Because..." said the Cat, "...it's fine."

The galleon descended gracefully, its anchor ring holding tight to the Travel Line and it eventually touched down softly in front of them. The gangplank slid down and Captain Thrace was standing at the top of it. He wasn't looking down at them, though – he was gazing into the distance, like he was trying to work out a particularly difficult piece of mathematics.

"Lady Eris is goin' to be lookin' fer me, ain't she?" he said into the crisp night air.

"Yup," the Cat answered, making himself comfortable ontop of a nearby wooden crate.

"The *Snake's* been used in two rescues off her island," Thrace said, "and she ain't likely to be too happy 'bout that, is she?"

The Cat shook his head as he lazily eyed a mouse scurrying past. "Not at all."

"Prob'ly got every Yarnbull, Sharp-Eye an' Needleman from Aquila to Zeon lookin' fer me."

"Well, let's put it this way…" the Cat looked at Captain Thrace at last. "There's a large target in the shape of Lady Eris' boot pasted right to your backside, Captain."

Thrace went quite pale.

"And how long do you think it'll take Lady Eris' people to find you?" asked the Cat, moving towards the *Snake*, now. "Well, I don't have to ask, do I? The fact that you came back here tells me you already came up with the answer."

Thrace nodded, his voice a little hoarse. "Not very long."

"And that's an optimistic estimate," said the Cat. He was now halfway up the gangplank. Teresa and Arthur, hadn't moved. The Cat continued. "Those other fellow prisoners of yours, they just did little things, didn't they? Said something bad about the Queen, maybe, or were at the wrong place at the wrong time. But you actually defied her, didn't you? Stole money from a ship owned by Lady Eris, I believe?"

"I didn't know it were hers…"

"Makes no difference. Lady Eris doesn't like to be defied. I know. I've been defying her for a long time. Of course, you *could* take your chances. Go on the run on your own."

"I've been on the run by meself fer me entire career!" the Captain tried to jut his chin out, defiantly.

"Ah, yes," said the Cat, almost at the top of the gangplank, "but you've never been on the run from Lady Eris. Trust me… that's a whole different game. Now, you can try and play that game by yourself…"

The Cat locked eyes with Thrace.

"…or you can stick with someone who knows how to win it."

Arthur could literally see the Captain's brain working it all out at super-speed. Trying to determine every possible way forward without the Cat. Arthur knew he'd soon work out that every single one of those ways forward had the same ending – him locked up in Eris' dungeons. If he was lucky.

But would that be enough, Arthur wondered? Captain Chadwell Thrace clearly liked being the master of his own destiny. He might still take the risk of going it alone. Unless…

"They're rich," Arthur suddenly said.

Thrace's gaze suddenly fixed on the young boy.

"Sorry?"

"The Queen, I mean. And Lady Eris," Arthur fumbled his way through, his nerve getting stronger as he went. "They're really, really rich. I mean, you already know that, don't you? Teresa tells me you tried to steal a few jewels. But imagine getting your hands on loads of it.

Enough to fill the hold of the *Snake* fifty times over. You wouldn't have to be a pirate anymore. You could buy your own island."

The idea seemed to light something behind the Captain's eyes. Arthur allowed himself a small smile as he dropped his final line on the old man.

"How do you fancy being called *Governor* Thrace?"

That sealed it. Arthur could tell by the look of yearning on the old man's face. Self-preservation was one thing.

Being ridiculously, filthy, stinking rich was quite another.

His eyes flicked between the Cat and Arthur.

Suddenly a great, warm smile erupted across the old man's face and he stood there, beaming at them, arms wide.

"Welcome aboard the *Gallopin' Snake*, me hearties! Congratulations – you're now a part o' me crew!"

The Cat grinned and strolled aboard. "Cheers."

Arthur and Teresa followed the Cat up. Teresa glared at Thrace as she went past, but said nothing. She still wasn't impressed that he'd tried to leave them behind, Arthur saw. He liked that she let him know it. Captain Thrace actually looked a little bit uncomfortable as he caught Teresa's gaze.

"Oh, one thing, Master Ness," Thrace suddenly took hold of Arthur's shoulder as he went by. "I'm not a pirate. I'm a businessman."

"Oh?" said the Cat. "And what's your business?"

"Piracy."

The Cat looked puzzled, "So… doesn't that make you a pirate, then?"

"Oh, no!" Thrace said, eyebrows raised. "That'd be where you're mistaken. See, a pirate sails around, stealin' things off of ships he comes across."

"And what do you do?"

"Me an' me crew ask all nice like if the folk on the other ship mind terribly if we relieve 'em of all their valuables."

"And if they say no?"

Thrace shrugged/ "Then we shoot 'em dead and take the valuables." He held up a finger, "But we *did* ask nice."

"Well," said the Cat, "far be it for the lowly crew to tell the Captain his business, but there won't be any of *that* going on anymore." The Cat fixed Thrace with a hard, threatening glare. "Am I making myself fabulously clear?"

Thrace made a slight bow. "I suppose so. There ain't nothin' wrong with a temporary change of approach..."

"Right then." The Cat sprang off down the deck, all sweetness and light again. "Get the gangplank up, you kids. The Captain is about to give us his first order."

"...I am?"

"Yes. You're about to order us to set sail for Bamboo's island."

"What..?" Thrace's eyes widened in surprise. "An' how are we goin' to find an island what can't be found on account it keeps *movin*?"

Arthur and Teresa looked on in shock. A moving island?

"Fortunately," said the Cat, "I've got directions."

Thrace looked about, clearly wondering just what he'd gotten himself into.

"Your orders, Captain?" asked the Cat. "Not that I'm trying to tell you what orders to give, of course, totally up to you. Your ship and all that."

Thrace paused for a moment. Arthur recognised the look on his face, because it was the same one he'd worn when he first met the Cat. The old man was trying to decide if he should follow the Cat out the window. Quickly, though, he made his decision.

"Teresa, Arthur, get that gangplank up, yer filthy gully-rats. Then Arthur, get yerself up that mast an' check the riggin'. Teresa, I need them rudder-wheels scrubbed an' locked then you're on the helm and waitin' for my instructions. Come on, get to it, yer bilge-eatin' maggots, we ain't got all day!"

He stalked off after the Cat. "Right, then, Cat, let's be havin' them directions. Bamboo's island awaits, so let's get goin'. The Queen's treasure ain't goin' ter steal itself."

A VISIT FROM A FRIEND
(from the busy thoughts of Montgomery Avis)

I have had the most exceedingly productive morning, here in the shop. Yes - *exceedingly* productive. Surely more productive than anyone else here on Graft. I make maps, you see. Absolute top quality, best of the best. And I've been working for weeks to try and manufacture a stronger type of map paper. This morning, I finally cracked it! The strongest, thinnest map paper in all Arilon!

The Queen may be flying around causing trouble, getting everyone hot under the collar and so on. But, at the end of the day, as my grandfather used to say, the more lost the world becomes, the more it will need maps to show it the way.

Ding-a-ling!

The shop door opens and in walks a fellow I haven't seen in ages.

"Mr Frogham!" I grin. "Why, my friend, it's been too long!"

"Yer right," says Frogham. "It has. I need to ask you something."

"Oh, straight down to business, as usual," I grin. "Not even going to ask me how come I'm never in the Broken Crown? Well, I shall tell you - it's the children, you see. Too noisy. They make my ears ache and-"

"Avis," Frogham interrupts, rudely. "I need one a' yer special maps. I need ter know how ter find Bamboo's Island."

Ah. Now, *this* could be awkward.

"Erm...well, the Cat told me never to tell anyone how to get there..." I stammer.

"Come on, Avis," Frogham smiles. "You can tell me. I'm one of the Cat's closest friends."

"Yes, I know," I say. "And as *you* well know, it's for that very reason, the Cat says you must never know. If the Queen ever wants information about the Cat, she'll try to capture his known friends and allies for interrogation. That means people like you, Andreyev Romanov, Big Sally and Little Sally... none of you can know. Me, on the other hand, well... nobody knows I'm the Cat's friend. So they won't come looking for me. It's quite safe for me to have that knowledge."

"These are dangerous times, Avis," says Frogham, darkly. "*No-one's* safe."

Ding-a-ling

The door opens again and in walk two men in dark suits, one carrying a small, black valise. I know straight away who they are. *What* they are. I turn and try to run out to the back of the shop - but a third man, identical to the other two, is already emerging from the back, blocking my way.

I turn back to Frogham. Except it isn't Frogam, is it? Frogham is gone. Gone somewhere no-one will ever be able to get him back from.

The Needleman with the valise takes a cotton mat out of it and lays it on the counter top. It has many blank faces - but two faces are filled in. Frogham's and someone else I don't recognise.

"I'll never talk!" I cry.

"You won't have ter," says the fake Frogham.

And the Needleman's fingers begin to move.

MAP GAZING

Arthur walked slowly and gingerly into the *Galloping Snake's* navigation room, the heavy mug of mudwater held carefully in both hands. The Cat and the Captain were studying a dizzying collection of maps and charts spread out over the large table.

At the sound of Arthur's entrance, Captain Thrace looked up.

"Ah, there ye are, lad!" the Captain bellowed. "I was beginnin' ter think ye'd gone all the way ter the Bog Islands to ferment the mudwater with yer own two hands!"

The Captain looked a lot different now, Arthur realised with a start. Dark britches, a crisp white shirt and all covered over by a long, black overcoat with gold trimmings. Still no eyepatch but at least there was a tri-corner hat. Now, he really *did* look like a pirate.

"Well, come on, lad! Before I die a' thirst!"

Arthur hurried over and Thrace took the tankard of brown, steaming liquid eagerly. Arthur, for his part, tried not to be sick as Thrace gulped down the horrid-looking stuff.

"Is it really from mud water? From a bog?" he asked, trying not to breathe in the smell.

"Don't judge, lad," said the Captain. "Properly filtered, mud water is a right tasty drink for real men of enterprise. Want to try some?"

"Not in a million years," Arthur said quickly. Captain Thrace and the Cat roared with laughter.

The Captain turned back to the table of charts. The Cat was reciting, from memory, a long, complicated string of co-ordinates that would help them find Bamboo's moving island. Arthur (not at all eager to get back to scrubbing the masthead) turned and looked around the rest of the room.

All over the walls, there were maps and charts and large sheets of paper with rows and rows of numbers on them. And dozens of shelves with rolled up tubes stacked higher than Arthur could reach. Arthur's eye soon landed on the biggest, oldest map of them all.

A map of Arilon.

Arthur moved slowly toward it, entranced by its size and detail. The paper was older and browner than anything else in the room and there were burn marks all around the edge. As Arthur got closer, he could see it wasn't printed but hand-drawn right onto the actual paper. It wasn't a mass-produced map, it was one of a kind. Some of the ink was old and nearly faded out. Other parts of it were darker, having been added more recently.

There were hundreds and hundreds of islands all connected by a countless mass of long, straight lines going in all directions. Each island's name was written beneath it and Arthur's eyes flitted from one to another, reading the strange names and trying to figure out what each island's Idea was.

Duseeya. Votum. Bonitas. But Arthur's eye was suddenly drawn to two islands that were sitting very close together, like twins.

"Phobos and Valia." The rough-as-sandpaper voice of the ship's captain came from just behind Arthur. Captain Thrace (thankfully minus the mudwater) pointed at the two islands on the map. "Phobos, the isle of Fear. And Valia. Isle of -"

"Bravery," Arthur whispered.

Arthur couldn't take his eyes off them. Either of them. After a moment, he turned to Captain Thrace, a little embarrassed.

"Sorry," he said. "It's just… it's an amazing map."

Beyond the Captain, Arthur saw there was no Cat. He must have ducked out for something. They were alone.

"Me father drew most of it," said the Captain, proudly. "I've added the odd bit here an' there. He travelled from one end of Arilon to the other, chartin' everything as he went. Used to tell me stories of all the things he'd seen. I swore I'd see 'em all meself one day. And most of 'em I have. Shardtree storms, Yarnbull fields, waterfalls tippin' off the edge of islands and fallin' away into the Black…"

He moved his head slightly toward Arthur and lowered his voice. "One time, I even saw the Rainhand."

"Rainhand?"

Thrace nodded and shivered at the same time. "Terrible, terrible creature. That's one experience I don't care to be repeatin'…"

"Is it still up to date? The map?" Arthur said, shaking the old man from his dark thoughts. "I mean, with the way the Queen gets rid of Travel Lines…"

Captain Thrace shrugged. "I s'pose I should get rid of it. Get meself one a' them fancy modern maps from Montgomery Avis or someone like that. Don't suppose me father would complain…"

Arthur looked up. "Oh… is he…?"

Thrace cut Arthur off. "Oh, no, he ain't dead. Well, not yet."

"So…why would he not mind if you threw out his map?"

Thrace was silent for a long time and Arthur began to wonder if he'd asked one question too far. Eventually, the old Captain spoke.

"He set sail from 'ome at sixteen. Before long, he got 'is own ship, the *Unicorn*. Went explorin' and adventurin' and everywhere he went, it were on that ship.

"While I were growin' up, each time the *Unicorn* came into port, I'd know I were goin' to get a present – some souvenir he'd brought back from some far-flung corner of Arilon. And I'd get stories of all the places he'd been and all the places he were goin' next. He must'a taken the *Unicorn* further away from the sun than anyone else ever.

"Then one day, the Queen cut a load a' Lines from Cassinus, the isle of adventure. Guess she didn't want people roamin' around, explorin'… just wanted 'em to have simple, borin' lives. Go to work. Go home. Nothin' else.

"Me father came back that very night. Set fire to the *Unicorn*. Made me burn every gift he'd ever bought me. Told me never to set foot on a ship. Then 'e went to bed. This map were the only thing what survived the *Unicorn* goin' up. I found it an' kept it hidden. Soon as I were old enough, I left home, took the map an' never looked back."

Captain Thrace turned to Arthur now, and whispered low and threatening into his ear. "Listen to me, lad, and listen good. There's lots a' things you can't control in this life. Why, the Queen could cut an island off tomorrow that'd make yer own mother stop lovin' you. So you make sure you look after yerself. Ferget ev'ryone else. If there's anythin' worth takin', then take it first, before anyone else. Whatever the cost."

And with that, he turned back to the chart table. The silence was heavy in the room and Arthur didn't know what to say. So he turned and left the old pirate on his own.

ARRIVAL AT BAMBOO'S ISLAND

Arthur stood at the front of the ship and watched Bamboo's Island slowly emerge from the darkness.

It was much smaller than Graft but bigger than Lady Eris' place. Whereas Graft looked like a town, this was more like a village. Instead of large spreads of buildings, it seemed Bamboo's Island had little clusters of huts dotted about here and there. Like they'd been sprinkled by some giant farmer's hand scattering corn on his fields.

As Arthur looked back and forth across the slowly enlargening island, his gaze caught the shiny, metal shape of the snake that formed the masthead at the very front of the ship. The figure that gave the *Galloping Snake* its name was stretched out in front of the vessel, its body, twirling and twisting around a long pole. The creature reached out ahead of the ship, hissing angrily at the skies. It looked to Arthur like something once alive, some kind of airborne serpent, frozen in mid-flight and placed on the front of this ship. It looked pretty angry, to be honest. He didn't fancy being around if it ever woke up.

"Prepare the gangplank, young Master Ness! This ain't a time fer lollygaggin'!" Captain Thrace's gravelly voice boomed out from the upper deck. Shaken from his thoughts, Arthur turned and jogged over to the starboard side of the ship.

"Aye, Captain!" he called back as he started to unlock the wooden walkway that they'd use to get on and off the ship once it landed.

"Keep us steady as she goes, Miss Smith!" he called to Teresa as she stood at the ship's wheel, guiding them down to the surface. Arthur noticed that she didn't reply with an 'Aye Captain'. Just a glare. To Arthur's surprise, Thrace didn't say anthing about it – he just gave a quick, uncomfortable cough and went off to talk to the Cat.

Arthur joined Teresa at the wheel.

"Still mad at the Captain, then?" he whispered to her.

She huffed as she glanced at him. "Stupid old man. Leavin' us behind like that."

"At least he came back."

"Only because he had to," Teresa said. "Only because he were scared of Lady Eris."

Why don't you tell her how scared you are, eh, Arthur?
How much you want to run away?

Filling the silence, Teresa said quietly. "Me mum died when I were really young. Not long after Sam were born. And me older brother, Albert, he's gone off to fight in the war." She kept her eyes firmly ahead, on the Travel Line before them. "I suppose I'm just not that good with people leaving me, that's all."

Tentatively, Arthur found himself putting a hand on Teresa's shoulder. She turned and looked at him. Arthur didn't say anything out loud, but from the touch on her shoulder and the look on his face, Teresa knew what he meant. He was promising to stick by her side. Whatever happened.

She smiled.

"Land, ho!" Captain Thrace called out from the main deck. Keeping the ship steady and slowly reducing the speed, Teresa brought them safely into the docks. They were a much smaller version of the ones on Graft. Only a couple of Travel Lines came to the island and there was just one other ship moored there. Finally, the *Galloping Snake* came to a stop with a small bump.

"Getting' better, eh?" Teresa said to Arthur with a wink. "Not dumpin' you on your backside anymore!"

Arthur laughed and ran down to the gangplank. Grabbing hold of the winch, he wound the handle round and round, the wooden walkway lowering itself with every turn. Soon, it had connected itself to the quayside.

"Right, everybody off!" called the Cat, striding down the gangplank. "Somebody remember where we parked."

The four members of the motley crew strode down to the quayside and there waiting for them was an old man standing next to a horse and trap cart. Arthur looked to the man as he expected some kind of greeting. A greeting did come, but not from the man.

"Hello, dearies!" said the horse. "My name's Mary! Welcome to Bamboo's Island! Hop onto my cart and we'll get going."

Arthur and Teresa exchanged surprised glances. Although they knew many animals in Arilon talked, it was the first time they'd actually been addressed by one other than the Cat.

In contrast, Captain Thrace and the Cat both jumped up onto the cart without a second glance. Teresa followed them. Arthur got on last, nodding to the old man who returned the nod with a heavy, weary one of his own.

The old cart creaked and bounced along, following a busy road out of the docks and into the evening countryside as they headed toward their destination village.

Arthur looked around him as nighttime began to creep, slowy across the landscape. The countryside was so like Waterwhistle with tall hills sloping down into large, expansive fields that ran for miles in all directions.

"I still can't imagine that all this is sitting ontop of a floating disc in space," he said to Teresa.

"I know what you mean," she replied. "But then, I suppose it's no different to everything on our planet being sat ontop of a ball floating in space."

"So, my dearies," the horse said, "let me welcome you again to Bamboo's Island. My name's Mary and this grumpy old man sat atop my cart is Elian. So, you're here to see Bamboo, are you? Well, that's just grand. Oh, yes, Bamboo can help you. I don't know what it is you're here to see him about, of course, none of my business, I'm just a lowly horse. But whatever it is, I'm sure you've come to the right place. Why, just last week Elian stubbed his toe on the kitchen table leg – oh, he was in a foul mood that day, let me tell you! And the *language--*"

"Horse, will you please just shut *up?!*" said the man, Elian, at last. "Crikey, it's a wonder you've any breath left in you after all your gossiping! And anyway, since when was this *your* cart?"

"Don't you 'shut up horse' *me*, you silly man," Mary whinnied back. "And of course it's my cart. I'm the one pulling it, aren't I? You just sit on it with your big, fat, backside. Sorry about that, people. My person's a bit grouchy."

"For the illionth time, I'm not your person, you're *my* horse!"

And so it carried on all the way through the countryside. Eventually, the Cat took mercy on everyone's ears and interrupted the squabbling couple, regaling them all instead with tales of his adventures and daring escapes from Lady Eris.

Before long, the cart trundled into a tiny village at the foot of a picturesque range of hills. The man and his horse (or the horse and her man) wound their way between the little bungalows and eventually dropped the group off outside a small, round hut in the centre of the village.

Outside, stood a young, dark-skinned boy in loose-fitting white and grey shirt and trousers. He looked a little bit like the Berber or Tuareg desert nomads Arthur had read about in the library.

"Welcome, my friends," said the boy, grinning as they pulled up. "Bamboo is waiting inside for you. Please, come with me."

Arthur followed the others clambering down off the cart.

"Bye, my dearies!" Mary called. "Hope you have a good visit!"

As they trotted away, Elian said something that sounded to Arthur like 'mind your own business, horse'. Mary argued something back but by now, the pair were disappearing into the rapidly descending darkness.

Arthur looked up into the sky and saw the island had rotated fully away from the sun now. As there was no moon, the only light came from the gas lamps that had somehow popped themselves on as the sunlight disappeared. Although he had already seen this on Graft, it seemed somehow more magical here since there were so few people and the whole village was just so peaceful and quiet.

A familiar nudge on his shoulder woke Arthur up.

"Hey, Captain Daydream," Teresa nodded to the door. "You comin'?"

Arthur took a deep breath. Okay. Time to go on the next stage of this wild ride.

"Time to see Bamboo," the Cat said as they entered the little hut. "Only thing I'll say… try not to stare."

"Stare?" Arthur asked. "At what?"

But the Cat just smiled.

BAMBOO

Arthur tried not to stare. He really did. He tried really very hard indeed. But he couldn't help it.

He was looking at a stick doll on a chair.

Teresa, not taking her eyes off the doll, leaned in close and whispered in Arthur's ear.

"So... Bamboo likes dolls? And this is...what? His favourite one?"

Behind the pair, Captain Thrace was slightly less subtle.

"You said, Cat, that Bamboo was crazy," he said in a gruff voice. "You never said he's a doll collector."

The Cat ignored Captain Thrace and stepped forward to the unmoving stick doll.

"Bamboo, my old friend," he said, "it's good to see you again."

Arthur looked about, puzzled. Why was the Cat addressing the doll? Some kind of strange Arilon custom?

The boy who had met them outside went over to the chair and bent his head down towards the doll's face. Arthur realised with some surprise that he appeared to be *listening* to the stick figure.

Presently, the boy stood up, smiled and spoke.

"Bamboo says he is so glad to see you alive, Cat," he said. "He had heard that the Queen had skinned you, turned you into a flag and flew you from the main mast of the *Twilight Palace*."

"Well, it wasn't quite the *main* mast," said the Cat, "just one of the smaller ones. Oh, but wait till you hear how I escaped..."

For the second time since landing on this island, Arthur and Teresa exchanged shocked glances – and this time, Captain Thrace joined them.

The *doll* was Bamboo?

The boy cocked his head again, listening to the tiny figure, even though it wasn't moving or speaking at all.

"Bamboo is very much looking forward to hearing about it," said the boy, "but time is very short and so will have to wait until another day. Before we begin, may I ask if anyone would like a glass of ice juice?"

"Tell the pile o' sticks over there that I'll have a tot o' rum," Captain Thrace was leaning on the back wall, arms crossed, an amused grin on his face.

The boy looked at the Captain. "Bamboo says you should not be so rude."

The Captain grinned wider. "Tell the pile o' sticks over there that I'm sorry."

The Cat interrupted with a warning glare at the Captain. "I think the drinks can wait, Bamboo. You're right – we're short on time. Please tell us the information you have on the Queen."

The boy nodded his head. "Of course. But first, Bamboo would like to speak to *him*."

The Cat was puzzled. "Who?"

Arthur's heart skipped a beat as the boy turned to look straight at him and pointed.

"Him. Bamboo would like a word with Arthur Ness."

THE CENTRE OF ALL THINGS

"I don't understand," said the Cat. "You know about Arthur?"

"Bamboo saw him in the Threads," said the boy. "He knew he was coming."

Arthur felt hot as everyone in the room turned to stare at him. Even the stick doll seemed to be looking right at him, knowingly.

The boy removed two pieces of paper from his shirt pocket.

"Have you explained to the human children what Bamboo is?" he asked the Cat.

Captain Thrace snorted, "You mean he *ain't* a pile of sticks on a chair?"

The Cat ignored the Captain and turned to Arthur and Teresa. "Bamboo is like the Queen and Lady Eris. He's a Weaver."

Arthur remembered hearing the Cat use that word when they were at the Broken Crown.

"What's a Weaver?" he asked.

"I suppose you'd say it's the same thing as being a wizard or a witch. Basically, its someone who has special abilities to manipulate the Threads. You've seen the huge Travel Lines that connect the islands? Well, just like them, all things, all people, all places are connected by invisible threads. Not just here, but in the Human World too. They connect you to your parents, your friends, your toys, places you like going..."

Arthur and Teresa exchanged sceptical glances.

"…invisible threads?" Teresa said in a voice that showed that Teresa and Arthur had switched the 'crazy' label from the stick doll to the talking cat.

The Cat simply smiled and went on. "Arthur, who's your best friend back home in London?"

Arthur thought – most of his friends back in London weren't very good friends. But there was one…

"Mickey."

"Well," the Cat explained, "when you and Mickey were born, a very thin, faint thread would have connected the two of you together. You see, even back then, there was a slim chance that you would grow up and meet each other. The older you got, the more events started to bring you together. Your parents moved to the same town, they sent you to the same school – each event made the thread that little bit thicker. Until eventually, you met one day - I'm guessing your first day of school?"

Arthur nodded.

"Well, when you met, the thread would have become very thick. And the closer friends you became, the thicker the thread grew. Until now you're best friends and it's as thick as your arm. It's the thing that makes you choose each other when it's playtime. It's the thing that will keep you writing to each other when you grow up and move apart."

Arthur nodded – he could what the Cat was saying. Some things in life, you felt more strongly about than others. Choosing one toy over another, one sweet over another, one person over another…

"And Bamboo can see these threads?" Arthur asked.

"Yes," the Cat nodded. "And through them, he can see how everything connects to everything else. From there, he can figure out certain things that might happen in the future."

"And so can the Queen?" Teresa asked, warily.

"Yes," said the Cat. "Very few people have that gift. They're all a little bit mad because of it." He turned to the doll and smiled, apologetically. "I hope you don't mind me saying..?"

The boy listened, grinned and said, "Bamboo says, no, not at all."

"Anyway," the Cat finished, "we're here because Bamboo has been reading the Threads and discovered important information about the Queen that he felt I needed to know."

The boy was silent for a long time as he listened to the unmoving doll. Eventually, he spoke.

"The Queen has been trying to gain control over everyone's thoughts for a long time now. A few people such as myself and the Cat have been able to fight against her. Fight... but not defeat. She has severed so many Travel Lines, most people are incapable of strong feelings of self-reliance, resistance or injustice. All feelings they would need to fight her. They are too scared. They are *letting* her win.

"But then, Bamboo noticed the threads were beginning to gather together. A new focal point was beginning to emerge from the chaos. The threads were showing him a person who would become extremely important in the fight against the Queen's tyranny."

Arthur felt a flush of anxiety as the boy returned his gaze to him.

"*You*, Arthur Ness," said the boy. "You are the key to defeating the Queen."

"Me..?" Arthur felt numb. "I'm going to defeat her?"

The boy shook his head. "Bamboo did not say you would defeat her – only that you are the key to doing so. If you turn one way, she is defeated. If you turn another, she will defeat *us*…"

"But…" Arthur's mouth was dry with shock, "…but I would never do that..! I'd never help her!"

But, even as he said the words, Arthur remembered how Lady Eris had tricked him into helping to grow the Yarnbulls in Waterwhistle. And he remembered how he suspected something was wrong – but he was so scared, he pretended everything was fine and went on helping her.

"Please remember, Arthur Ness," the boy said, his voice calm and serene, "nothing is for certain. The threads simply show what *might* happen. What is *likely* to happen. But the only ones who can control what *will* happen is *us*. We have to make our own choices and do what we feel we must."

Arthur suddenly felt like he was under some unbelievable, massive weight.

"Why me?" he asked, his voice a little hoarse. "I'm not special."

"You may not have been born special," said the boy, "but circumstances *made* you special. You're just the right person in the right place at the right time."

Yes, Arthur thought, or the wrong person at the wrong place at the wrong time…

Arthur's head was spinning. He looked at the Cat for some help but the Cat simply stared back at him, completely without expression.

"What is it you want most, Arthur Ness?" the boy asked, softly.

"To not be scared all the time," Arthur said immediately, "...and to go home."

"If you wish to go home, simply ask," said the boy. "There are many tapestries and woven rugs in the Human World and in Arilon that serve as gateways to one another. All you need is to possess the power to step through them, as the Cat does. The nearest such portal is back on the island of Graft."

The boy handed Arthur one of the pieces of paper he was holding. "This is a spell-map that will open that portal and take you to the rug in the hallway of your home in London."

Arthur almost fell over in shock. This crazy stick doll (or crazy boy – he wasn't sure anymore who it was that was crazy) had just handed him a way home! Not to Waterwhistle, but to his actual, actual home in London – to his mother!

"You may leave whenever you wish," said the boy. "The Cat will help you."

Arthur looked back at the Cat who simply nodded, silently. His face was still expressionless. Arthur felt the weight of all the eyes in the room on him. They were waiting for his decision.

Do it! Do it now!
You know you want to run far away from here!
They're giving you the chance! Take it!

Arthur wanted to listen to his fear. He really did. He could almost see the black and white tiles on the hallway floor back home. And smell the varnish on the coat rack that his father had built just before going away. And see his mother, coming to greet him, smiling, arms open wide...

Then Arthur glanced across at Teresa. For the first time since he met her, she actually looked scared. And he remembered his unspoken promise to her.

"I... er..." Arthur mumbled at first, but then cleared his throat and spoke up louder, "I want to stay and help you fight against Lady Eris and the Queen."

Arthur folded up the spellmap and put it into his pocket.

You're going to regret that...

He'd said the right thing, hadn't he? It felt good to say it, didn't it? Teresa and the Cat were smiling at him now. Yes, he decided. It was the right thing to say.

We'll see, scaredy-cat...

"Very well," said the boy, "and so, onto the Queen. As we know, the Queen has been trying to control everyone's thoughts and feelings by cutting the Travel Lines. But, slowly, the Queen has realised the truth – cutting the Lines greatly influences what people feel but it cannot control their thoughts completely. And so she has begun a new plan.

"The Queen is building a machine."

THE AGENCY ENGINE

"A…machine?" the Cat repeated, wide-eyed. Arthur could tell from the Cat's tone that this was an unexpected move for the Queen. Something the Cat hadn't seen from her before.

From the rear of the room, Captain Thrace snorted, "A machine? Is that what you folk are all worryin' about? Just take a hammer to it and smash it to pieces. Job done, let's go for a beer."

"And how do you smash a machine as big as Arilon?" the boy said to the old Captain. "How do you smash a machine that stretches from one side of the NothingSpace to the other? How do you destroy a machine that has a piece, a pipe, a cable in every island, in every building, in every room, in every man, woman and child in all of Arilon?"

Silence. Everyone was stunned.

"That's a big machine," the Captain admitted.

"Such a huge thing in the hands of the Queen…" the Cat whispered in awe. "What is it for, exactly?"

"Usually, when Bamboo reads the Threads," the boy said, "they point towards some idea or purpose. But around this machine, the threads simply…stop. Nothing can penetrate. Its very existence blocks any potential reading of the future. The only thing that has emerged is the machine's name," the boy paused. "The Queen calls it the Agency Engine."

The instant the boy said the name, the mood in the room changed. The words hung in the air like a guillotine blade waiting to drop. Nobody knew what the name meant – but it was as if upon hearing it, everyone instinctively knew it meant their doom.

Eventually, the boy spoke again.

"The Threads did not show Bamboo how the machine will work exactly. But knowing the Queen, he feels it must be for one end and one end alone," the boy fixed his gaze on the Cat. "Control. The Queen will use it to do the only thing she has ever wanted to do. Take control of everyone, everywhere. Forever."

Everyone sat still for a moment more. And Arthur was already beginning to regret his decision not to leave when he'd had the chance.

"You said it stretches right across Arilon," said the Cat, "but the good Captain is right… It must have a physical location. A place we can actually go to somehow destroy it."

"Bamboo believes that it does," said the boy, "but where that is, he cannot yet tell. However, although the main machine itself is still some distance from full completion, there is one, small part of it that is almost done.

"This part of the machine alone will have the ability to grant power to the Queen such as we have never seen before. If it is activated, no-one will be able to stand against her and prevent her from completing the rest of the Agency Engine. And so, it is this small part which you must put all your energies into stopping for now."

"So tell us, lad…" Captain Thrace leaned forward, taking everything more seriously now, "…where might this part be found?"

The boy cocked his head, listening to the doll and then spoke again.

"Bamboo cannot be sure. It is very difficult to read anything in the Threads directly about the machine. However, they have shown him the location of someone who does possess the knowledge we seek. The machine's creator."

The boy finally presented the second piece of paper he'd been holding. He unfolded it and showed a grainy-looking photo to his audience.

"His name is Zane Rackham," the boy said. "He is a genius. For years, he worked at the University on Doctreena. He was one of its top professors – and its youngest ever. But one day, a couple of years ago, he disappeared."

The Cat nodded. "I remember. We thought the Queen had taken him but we didn't know what for."

"But now we do," said the boy. Captain Thrace took the photo from the boy and looked at it, closely. Turning it over, he read the information about Zane Rackham on the back.

"Says here, he's been arrested by peace keepers," said the Captain with raised eyebrows. "For bein' drunk an' disorderly in the streets. I like 'im already."

"Okay…" the Cat took a guess, "…so he got abducted, the Queen forced him to design this terrible machine and then he escaped."

"And then got drunk?" Teresa asked, suspiciously.

"Maybe it was because it was his first night off in years," the Captain sneered.

"Or maybe," said the Cat, "he was feeling guilty about what he'd done."

"Regardless, he is now being held by peacekeepers on the isle of Labyrinth," said the boy. "But Bamboo has seen in the Threads that even as we speak, the Queen's agents are on their way to recapture him. If you are to learn anything about the Agency Engine, you must get to him before they do."

"Labyrinth?" the Captain snorted. "That's over a hundred leagues from here!"

The boy smiled. "Then it is fortunate that Bamboo also saw Threads connecting the Cat to an old, selfish pirate who was Captain of the fastest ship in the Black."

Captain Thrace clearly didn't know whether to be offended at being called selfish or complimented on the *Snake* being the fastest vessel in Arilon. In the end, he just shifted uncomfortably and said;

"I ain't a pirate. I'm a businessman."

"Yes..." the boy smiled, "...who specialises in piracy."

ARTHUR THE COWARD
(from the secretive thoughts of the Cat)

Well. *That* was interesting.

The Agency Engine.

Well, Queenie, this is a new type of move for you. Bold. It feels like a winner-takes-all kind of play. I don't like it – mainly because it looks like you're already several moves ahead of me. And that just won't do.

"Did you know, I've been everywhere on this island?" chats Mary as our strange, little group trundles back towards the docks. It's the middle of the night, now. Fully dark. Only the comforting glow of gas lamps to light our way.

"Excuse me!" says poor Elian. "I've *driven* you everywhere on this island!"

"And I've carried you everywhere on this island," Mary huffs. "Which means I've done twice the distance."

"You've certainly done twice the talking."

"Yes..." says the horse, "...and twice the thinking. And judging by how heavy this carriage is getting to pull, you've definitely been doing twice the eating."

"And judging by how much my ears ache, you've been doing twice the moaning."

I never get tired of hearing these two bicker. I've met them several times but they never remember me. They're too wrapped up in their own world to take much notice of all the big, strange, dangerous things going on around them. They pretend to get on each others' nerves but truth be told, neither of them would have it any other way.

In a funny kind of way, I think they're probably the happiest beings I've ever met.

Unlike Arthur.

He's barely said a word since we left Bamboo's place.

I lean close. "I'll bet when you followed me out of that window, you never thought you'd end up talking to a stick doll in a chair."

Arthur looks at me with some surprise. "So, he really is just a stick doll, then?"

"Of course he is."

Arthur sits back. "I knew he wasn't alive."

"Arthur, Arthur, Arthur – just because he's a stick doll," I smirk, "doesn't mean he isn't alive."

Teresa gazes up into the starless sky, shaking her head, slowly. "I just can't believe it."

"I know…" I say, "…once you've spoken to a talking doll, a talking cat is just old news. I feel so out of date."

"No, I mean all this trouble, everything what Lady Eris and the Queen are doin' to Arilon. And now they want to come over and do it to me and Arthur's world, too."

"We *will* stop her," I say, trying to sound as reassuring as I can. "I'm rather good at stopping her, you know. I've done it loads of times before."

"She didn't have the Agency Engine before," Arthur says.

I can't argue with him on that.

"But, you're right, Cat," says Teresa. "We're still in the game. As long as we keep fightin', there's always a chance. Right, Arthur?"

Arthur looks at her and a kind of confidence seems to fill him. He smiles a determined smile.

"Right," he says.

I nod and smile at the pair of them. But I'm worried. Yes, it's a kind of confidence Arthur seems to be showing. But it's the wrong kind. The kind you put on because you think you should. The kind you try to feel for the benefit of someone else. Instead of the real kind – the kind you feel from deep inside.

Now, sure, pretend confidence is better than no confidence at all... but...

Well, it's like wearing someone else's coat. Fine, it'll keep you dry in the rain for a little while. But pretty soon, you'll realise it's just not your size. Too big or too small. Too long in the arms. Too tight round the shoulders. And it won't protect you from the rain as well as you thought it would. You'll realise that coming out in the rain with someone else's coat was a big mistake. Without your own coat, one that fits you just right, you'll just get yourself into all kinds of bother and...well...

You find that it's just better for all concerned if you'd just stayed at home.

"Thank you for staying behind, Cat," the boy – Bamboo's Voice – says after Thrace, Teresa and Arthur head outside to wait for our ride back to the docks. "Bamboo would like a word with you before you leave."

"I know," I say, glancing over to the motionless doll. "You want to talk about Arthur, don't you?"

The boy listens for a moment and then says, "Arthur Ness... he is full of fear."

"Yes," I say. "He's been like that since I met him.

He thinks of himself as a coward."

"He does not know the truth about bravery?"

I shake my head and sigh. "Nope. And I can't tell him. He has to figure it out for himself. He'll never believe it if it comes from someone else."

The boy pauses and then says, very slowly, very deliberately, "Bamboo was not entirely truthful before. The threads around Arthur Ness are somewhat clearer than he wanted to say in front of everyone."

I don't think I'm going to like the sound of this.

"There will be several times when Arthur must make the right choices and face his fears. One of them will happen very soon. If Arthur's courage fails him and he makes the wrong choice…"

He pauses. I say nothing and force him to spell it out.

"Lady Eris will capture you all," he says, eventually. "And the Queen will win."

I was right. I don't like the sound of that at all.

THE CORNER OF YOUR EYE
(from the defiant but scared thoughts of Sam Smith)

Sam kicked his legs and swung back and forth on the playground swing. He did it just like the other children did. Slowly. Evenly. Without smiling. He did everything to make sure he looked just like every other child in Waterwhistle.

And yet, the five Yarnbulls at the gates of the park were not staring at any other children. They were only staring at him.

The girl on the swing next to Sam was beginning to slow down so Sam stopped kicking too, allowing his swing to do the same. Gradually, and at the same rate as May Nicholls, Sam's swing came to a stop. He glanced across at her, briefly.

May was staring straight ahead, as usual. She could see what was there, in front of her but, somehow, she also couldn't. There was a look in her eyes. Not exactly lifeless, there was definitely something there. It was just that she'd been kind of... paused.

She used to be the loudest person in Sam's class. Girl or boy, it didn't matter, May Nicholls outdid them all for noise. She was always at the centre of everything, the life of the classroom. The other kids called her May-May because it seemed like there was always two of her, so involved she was in everything going on.

There wasn't two of her anymore. There was barely even one of her.

She stepped off her swing and Sam did the same. He followed her to the gates of the park, doing his best to copy the way she walked. No enthusiastic bounce, no skipping, no running. Just a simple, languid movement. Like a puppet being moved by a puppeteer who was himself lifeless.

May passed through the gates and between the Yarnbulls. None of them even glanced in her direction.

They were all watching Sam.

As he walked between them, Sam couldn't stop his heart thumping faster and faster. He'd become well practiced at pretending not to see the Yarnbulls. He kept his eyes fixed on something in the distance – like a window or a wall – and he simply used his peripheral vision to avoid bumping into things. As best as he could figure, that was how everyone else in the village was, anyway. Some outside part of their vision could see the Yarnbulls, that's why they never bumped into them. It was the central part of their vision – and their minds – that ignored them.

So, yes, Sam could move in just the right way, look just the right way and sound just the right way...

But he was still terrified.

The tall, dark creatures stared down at the child as he walked between them. Their massive, horned heads turned to follow him as he passed. Apart from that, they were completely still, like statues. Their huge hands held their weapons motionless at their sides.

And soon, Sam had passed through the group and was heading down the lane. He didn't dare turn back to look at them. If he did such a foolish thing, they'd be upon him in an instant. So he kept his eyes fixed on his father's shop, right at the end of the road, and walked slowly towards it.

He didn't even turn his head when not-quite-whole May turned up Lamb Lane and wandered off towards her house.

Before long, though, Sam was back home, preparing the evening meal for when his father got in. Even at home, Sam didn't dare let his guard down. More than once, he'd looked up only to find a Yarnbull staring silently in from the other side of a closed window. In those situations, he had to work very hard to hide his shock. Failure to do so would have resulted in the Yarnbull smashing through the glass and reaching in for him right then and there.

No sooner had Sam taken the potatoes off the boil than the front door scraped open. Father was home.

As Sam placed the food on the table, he could hear a coat being removed and hung on the peg out in the hallway. Then boots being taken off and left by the door and slippers being shuffled on.

And then, silently as always, Mr Smith entered the room, sat at the table and began to eat.

"Get some salt, Sam," he said, finally, between mouthfuls. Sam did as he was asked and left the salt just in front of his father. Mr. Smith looked up for the first time since entering the room in order to pick up the salt shaker. That's when he noticed it.

"What's that?" he said.

Sam, who had returned to his seat and continued eating, didn't look up. He simply said;

"What?"

"That," said his father. "You've set an extra place."

Sam looked up. Yes he had. On purpose. He looked up at his father. He stared into his eyes. He searched for the slightest glimpse, the merest spark that something was wrong. That he could remember that, yes, there should indeed be three of them.

"Put it away," Mr Smith said. And went back to eating.

"But..."

"Put. It. Away." His tone warned that this conversation was over.

Defeated, Sam moved slowly towards the plate and cutlery. Wordlessly, he picked them up. He watched his father continue to eat and suddenly noticed something that took him by surprise. A small tear in the corner of his father's eye.

He knows, Sam thought. Surely, surely, he knows. Out of his peripheral vision. Out of the corner of his eye. He knows something's wrong. He knows his daughter's missing.

And in that moment, Sam felt joy for the first time in ages. Yes, when he'd spoken to Arthur, he'd felt hope. But now, he felt actual joy. Because he knew something of his father was still there.

And that's when, with a mighty **BOOM**, the front door flew into the room, right off its hinges. Sam did his best not to look up but that didn't stop a procession of Yarnbulls streaming into the house, reaching towards him with their huge, monstrous hands.

THE CORNER OF YOUR EYE

(from the befuddled thoughts of Mr. Smith)

Mr Smith munched on a bit of carrot and gravy and looked up. Strange. Why was there a smashed plate on the floor beside him? And the door was off its hinges. Maybe he'd left it open when he'd come in and the wind had blown it right off. Yes, that must have been it. And it had made him jump, which is why he'd knocked that plate on the floor. Yes, that made sense.

And then he'd started eating his dinner. Of course. He must have decided to fix it all after he'd finished eating. No sense letting his food get cold. He was about to go back to his potatoes when he noticed something that made his brow furrow in bemusement.

There was a half-eaten plate of food at the other side of the table. Why was that there?

But of course, the answer came to him, he must have left it there from last night. Too exhausted after a day's hard work to finish his own dinner.

Yes, there was an answer to everything. Contented, he went back to his food.

As he ate, he felt something trickle out of his eye and down his cheek. A tear? Why was there a tear coming out of the corner of his eye? It wasn't as though he felt sad in any way. No aching sense of loss, no despair. He felt fine.

He wiped the tear away and forgot about it.

LABYRINTH

Arthur, Teresa and the Cat stared in open-mouthed disbelief.

"Arthur?"

"Yes, Cat?"

"You know that map I just had you draw?"

"Yes, Cat?"

"Tear it up and throw it away, there's a good lad."

"Yes, Cat."

As the Cat and Captain Thrace had explained to the two human children, the island of Labyrinth was basically a huge maze. The streets and lanes twisted unnecessarily in hundreds of different directions and crossed each other thousands of times over. To get from one end of a street to the other was never a straight line. In fact just walking down the road was a good way to get very, very lost.

Ontop of that, every single street, path, road and avenue was lined down each side with wide, open gaps. The fissures went all the way to the underside of the island and the NothingSpace was clearly visible through them. In short, if you tried to cheat and cut across paths, you fell straight into the Black.

Regular people lived and worked on Labyrinth and they all embodied the island's Idea – dealing with complex paths. They knew that life could sometimes look very complicated and tricky and if you panicked and ran about, you'd make yourself lost and confused. However, if you kept calm and evaluated your surroundings, you would always, eventually find your way out of trouble.

Because of the nature of the place, it was the perfect spot to build a prison and so the peace keepers had done just that. Labyrinth Prison was a huge facility and sat right in the centre of the island. It was filled with criminals from all over Arilon. It didn't matter if people escaped the building – they would never be able to escape the island. Not before the peace keepers caught up with them.

All this was already known to the trio when they had left the *Galloping Snake* moored up at the docks under the guard of her Captain. And the Cat had been here enough times in the past that he had memorised the path to the prison. One hastily drawn map later and the three would-be jailbreakers had been confident of an easy stroll to the jailhouse to find Zane Rackham.

Unfortunately, very few things in life end up being as easy as they seem at the start.

"I take it those things weren't here the last time you came, then, Cat?" asked Teresa.

"You take it right, Smithy. And you know what? It's just not fair. Not fair at all."

Arthur walked up close to the thing they were staring at. The thing that had thrown such an early spanner into the works.

It was a tall, wooden archway that spanned the entire width of the road they stood on. To go any further along the street, you had to pass under it. However, the street they could see on the other side of the archway was not the street they were standing on.

What they could see was a road in another part of the island entirely. There was a tall, crimson tower right next to them with a banner advertising labouring work at the docks. Impossibly, as they looked through the archway, they could see that very same tower far off in the distance.

In other words, if you walked through the archway, you would instantly be transported to a road on the other side of the island. What was worse, Arthur could see even more archways dotted along the street, all no doubt leading to various random streets all over Labyrinth. They were everywhere.

And that wasn't all.

Every few seconds, the destination on the other side of the archway changed, like a radio channel being constantly flicked over. One moment, you could see a long, main road. Then the picture suddenly changed to a small side-alley. A few moments later, it was a row of houses. Seconds later again, it was the driveway of a busy office block.

"How are we supposed to find our way through all that…?" Teresa did not sound impressed one bit. "It's bad enough the island's roads are more twisted than a plate of drunken worms and there are gaps of NothingSpace everywhere… now we have to figure out magical, changing doorways too?"

"It's like playing snakes and ladders," said Arthur. "But with no ladders. And snakes that eat you and steal your money."

"This is a big delay we don't have time for," said the Cat. "The Queen's soldiers will be on their way right now. We need to get to Rackham before they do."

Arthur tried to clear his mind and figure this problem out, just like the people of Labyrinth would do. He took a deep breath and squinted against the bright Arilon morning. He didn't think he'd ever get used to the bizarre nature of daytime in Arilon. The top of the island was currently rotated towards the sun so a harsh, white light filled the island – and yet the sky was still black.

Arthur brought his gaze back down again to the streets around him. He watched as an older man in an expensive-looking outfit and carrying a large pile of papers strolled through the archway before them. He left the busy docks behind him and headed into a long street filled with houses. No sooner had he done that than the view of the houses disappeared. The archway now showed a high street, thick with horse-drawn carts going to market. One of the carts rolled out of the archway and trundled past the trio.

"The locals!" Arthur exclaimed all of a sudden. The other two looked at him, surprised at his sudden animation. Arthur carried on. "Look at them..! They know just when the doorways will change and what they'll change to."

"Hey, you're right..." Teresa looked about and saw people standing patiently in front of an archway as it flicked from street to path to lane before they eventually stepped through as it cycled round to their desired location.

"So...we'll just get one of them to help us." Teresa smiled. "I'm sure it shouldn't be too hard."

"Good luck with that," the Cat said, shaking his head. "The Queen has cut so many Travel Lines from Savis, the kindness island, most people just don't help strangers anymore. They'll probably just walk right past. You'd need to find someone extraordinarily naturally kind and the chances of that are roughly zer-"

"Excuse me, are you three lost?" an old lady's voice suddenly came from behind them. The three visitors turned to see an elderly woman holding an umbrella in one arm

- 167 -

and a tiny dog in the other. "Oh, dear," she smiled a kindly smile. "You look even more lost from the front! Why don't you tell me where you're headed, dearies. Perhaps I can help."

Teresa spared a gloating glance for the Cat before replying to the old lady. "Oh, thanks, ma'am. We're... erm... looking for the prison."

"Right you are," the lady said. "None of my business what you need the prison for. Just be careful, that's all I'll say. Some very unsavoury characters in there, you know. You're in luck, though. I live on the other side of the prison and I'm going home right now. Come on. Follow me."

A KIND OF KINDNESS

The old lady's name was Mila Evansworth. Her tiny dog was of the non-talking variety. It was named Trevor. She lived on Astrid Street in District Seventy-Two in a lovely little bungalow. Her mother and father had moved here from Graft and Elysium respectively when they were newlweds because her father had managed to get a job at a bank on Labyrinth. Her favourite colour was Sunset Red.

This and a hundred other things Arthur, Teresa and the Cat learned about the old lady as she led them through archway after archway and street after street. She didn't stop nattering the entire time.

"...and of course my parents had already said I wasn't allowed to go but all my friends were going, you see. And the High-Tones weren't going to tour again so this would be my last chance. I'd heard so much about them but I'd never actually heard any of their music. You see, I'd been ill when-"

"I'm sorry, are you sure this is the quickest way to the prison?" The Cat politely interrupted Mila's story. "Only, we're in a bit of a rush."

"Oh, yes, dear." Mila nodded. "I've walked up and down these streets more times than you've had hot dinners. This is definitely the most direct path. This route used to be a regular one of mine. I used to date a guard from the prison, you see. And we'd both love to go to the docks and watch the ships come and go. Of course, that was before the archways were put in. But once they'd been here a while, you soon got used to them as long as you were patient. Ooh, not like young Franklin Winterbottom. Now there was an impatient so-and-so. And ever so *tall!* You know, once, about fifteen years ago, he…"

Teresa leaned close to Arthur and whispered, "Crikey, there ain't no stoppin' her, is there? She's like a chatterbox tank!"

Arthur grinned. "Remind you of a certain talking horse?"

"I wonder if Trevor really is a non-talkin' animal?" Teresa whispered. "Or if he just can't get a word in and has given up tryin'."

The pair stifled a laugh as they passed under another archway that took them from a tree-lined park into a grey, dingy part of town. Trees, bushes and grassy spaces gave way to ugly, depressing-looking, concrete buildings with tiny windows. The buildings encircled one structure that was more ugly and more depressing-looking than the rest of them put together.

"And here we are," came Mila's cheery voice. "The centre of the island. Labyrinth Prison!"

Arthur had expected some kind of super-tall tower block stretching up into the sky. He was half right. It was very, very tall, but instead of going up, it went down. It had been lowered into a huge, circular gap in the island's floor and was suspended over the NothingSpace. A series of bridges and struts fanned out from the building like hands of a clock and it was by these that the building clung to the island.

It was abundantly clear there was no way in or out of that place except along one of those bridges because with nothing but a long drop into the Black beneath them, prisoners were certainly *not* going to be climbing out of any windows.

"Now, listen, dears." Mila turned to them. "Do you want me to wait for you? I don't mind!"

The Cat stepped up to the old lady. "Mila Evansworth, you've done more than enough for us already. We can't ask you to-"

"Oh, don't be silly!" Mila gave a dismissive wave of her hand. "Without learning the sequences of the archways, you could be wandering these streets for months, if not years! And people round here aren't as friendly as they used to be thanks to... you know... *her*."

Arthur knew just which 'her' Mila meant. Just as he knew that they were lucky to have bumped into this lady. There can't have been many people who would have been as willing to help strangers the way she had. Arthur glanced at Teresa and could tell she was thinking the same thing. They were both feeling a little guilty at making fun of her earlier. With all the Queen's pruning of Travel Lines, people as kind as Mila Evansworth were in danger of becoming extinct.

"Madam," said the Cat, bowing low, "you are one in a million. We'll be two shakes of a lamb's tale, I promise."

"Oh, don't worry about me." Mila settled herself down onto a nearby bench. "I've got Trevor to keep me company until you get back. Did you know that he-"

Ami Stark craned her eyes skyward as all around her, people began to cry out in fear and panic. Some pointed up, some ran about, some gathered up their little ones and whisked them away inside the nearest

---

building. But Ami didn't move. She just watched the *Twilight Palace* emerge out of the Black and sail down towards her home.

Everyone on Savis knew what it meant. The Queen's flagship had been to the island twice before. Her most recent visit just eight months ago. Each time, the Nightmare Ship and its fleet of fighter craft had cut hundreds of Travel Lines. With less than two hundred Lines left, many of the island's inhabitants had packed up their valuables and fled, fearing the Queen's inevitable return.

Ami had berated them and called them cowards. Now, as she stood and watched the Queen's flagship descend towards her home once more, she had to suspect those others had had the right idea after all.

The panicked, fearful cries of the people around her rose to a new crescendo as everyone watched the massive cutting blades slowly unfold from the underside of the *Twilight Palace*, their pristine sheen glinting in the bright midday sun.

Ami Stark grew fearful. Not for herself. Not for the other inhabitants of her island. But for the people out there on Arilon's other islands. Because right now, the Queen's selfishness was again changing minds.

All of a sudden, the old lady stopped talking. Arthur and Teresa watched in bewilderment as both Mila and the Cat staggered a little. It was as if they'd briefly been about to faint. The moment passed swiftly but something was undeniably different, now. When Mila spoke again, she wasn't the Mila Evansworth they had met. That Mila was gone and a new version of her stood in her place.

"Why am I helping you?" she said, her voice suddenly cold and hostile. "You're nothing to do with me! Helping you doesn't get me anything."

She suddenly stood up, the human children's shocked gaze following her.

"I'm off home," she said, gruffly, turning to go, not even looking at Arthur or the others. "You're on your own."

And with that, Mila Evansworth shuffled off down the road. She passed through an archway and the very next second, it changed to another location. She was gone.

Teresa crossed her arms. "Well, that were just *rude!*"

"Are you okay?" Arthur asked the Cat. "What happened?"

The Cat took a moment to compose himself. When he eventually looked up at Arthur, there was something different in his eyes. Just for a second.

"The Queen," he said. "She's at Savis. Kindness just became even harder to come by in Arilon."

"We're never going to find anyone to help us get back, then, are we?" Teresa said. "It's almost like the Queen knew we were goin' to be here."

The Cat glanced at her for a moment. "Wouldn't surprise me. Don't forget, she's a Weaver, too, just like Bamboo. Come on, we'd better get a move on. We don't have much time."

ZANE RACKHAM

The trio walked along one of the massive bridges holding the prison onto the island. As they approached the large, imposing main entrance, they passed a sign noting that the Guards' Stables were located a short distance down a side-path.

"See that sign?" the Cat said.

Teresa nodded. "Stables? So?"

"First rule of an amazing escape," the Cat smiled. "Never enter a place you can't leave *really* fast."

Arthur understood – the Cat paid attention to *everything*.

The three would-be prison visitors finally entered the low-ceilinged reception area. They found themselves in a circular room with a desk in the middle at which sat an officious-looking young man in a dark blue uniform. Behind him was a row of doors labelled 'Gate 1' all the way up to 'Gate 7'.

"Yes, can I help you?" the man said in a nasally-voice as the Cat approached the desk. He sounded very much like he didn't want to help them at all.

"I'm here to see Zane Rackham," said the Cat.

"You have an authorisation code, I assume?"

"Gamma Eight Seven," replied the Cat.

The man ran his finger down one of his sheets of paper, looking for the code. After a few seconds, he raised an eyebrow.

"Ah, here it is," he said, "Gamma Eight Sev-" He suddenly stopped, mid-sentence. His eyes widened in surprise and he went a worrying shade of white. "G-Gamma Eight Seven..?" he repeated. And then he did something that Arthur and Teresa were definitely not expecting. He stood up and saluted.

"My apologies, your Highness," he stammered, "...of course, sir, you may see who you like, sir. Would you like an escort, sir?"

"Oh, don't bother with any of that stuff," the Cat said with a dismissive wave of his paw. "Just tell me where Prisoner Rackham's holed up and we'll be on our way."

"Of course, sir," the man bumbled and flicked through several sheets of paper before finding what he was after. "Level 18, Sector 5, Cell 22. Use Gate 3. It's a low security cell, sir. Says here he was picked up for being drunk and disorderly but he's a bit... well, not quite right, sir. If you know what I mean."

Arthur did not know what he meant and judging from her expression, neither did Teresa. The Cat, however, simply nodded.

"Thank you, young man. And may I say, you have excellent manners. Come along, non-cats."

And off he headed towards the far wall where the door to Gate 3 was automatically opening for them. The three of them stepped through the door and Arthur realised they were actually in an elevator. Next to the open door, a large, brass dial sat surrounded by a ring of numbers. In the centre of the dial was a green, metal button marked with an arrow.

"Level 18 please, Smithy," said the Cat. Teresa twisted the dial to point at 18 and pushed the arrow button and the lift lurched into motion. As the carriage jarred and bumped slowly downwards, all three stood without talking.

Only the winding and occasional creak of the carriage broke the silence. Eventually, Arthur spoke.

"Okay, shall I go first?" he said.

The Cat blinked up at him. "Hm, I'm sorry?"

"Your highness...?" Arthur was flabberghasted. "Your *highness?*"

"Oh, that." The Cat sniffed and turned back toward the elevator door. "I used to be a King. Sorry, didn't I mention it?"

"Let me think..." Teresa said, sarcastically, "...flyin' ships...Travel Lines...evil Queens...no, no I don't think it came up."

"Well, it's not something I like to boast about. As you know, I'm a very modest fellow, I don't really like to brag," the Cat said, casually. "I'm sure I'd have worked my way round to it eventually. Ah, here we are."

The lift bell chimed and the elevator doors opened. The Cat slipped out, leaving Arthur and Teresa still staring after him, dazed.

"Impossible, impossible creature." Teresa shook her head.

"Do you ever get the feeling..." Arthur started. His tone was suddenly quiet and secretive which instantly intrigued Teresa and she turned to him. "...I don't know..." Arthur went on, "...do you ever get the feeling that he isn't completely honest with us about things..?"

"I suppose..." Teresa shrugged. "But I still trust him."

So do I, Arthur thought, *that's the problem.*

"Keep up, non-cats!" the voice called to them from down the corridor and the pair quickly caught up with the apparently royal feline, leaving the elevator door closing slowly behind.

"Second rule of an amazing escape," the Cat said. "Anyone want to take a guess what it is?"

Teresa and Arthur looked at each other and shrugged. The speed that the feline could change topic of conversation baffled them.

Seeing their empty stares, the Cat sighed and pointed with his nose toward a ventilation shaft high up on the wall. "Check to see if you can fit into places you're not meant to go," he grinned.

The children both stared at the shaft entrance. It was big enough for the Cat but way too small for them.

"Ah, here we are," said the Cat from a short way down the hall. "Enter Gamma Eight Seven into that dial will you, Arthur, there's a good lad."

The pair caught up with the Cat and Arthur saw the number 33 on the cell door in front of them. Under the number was fastened a piece of paper upon which was scribbled, 'Zane Rackham'. Next to it was another dial with numbers and letters in concentric circles running around it. Arthur turned the dial slowly and carefully so that it pointed to each part of the Cat's code, pressing the central button each time. Upon confirming the 'Seven', the door suddenly **clanked** open.

"Right," said the Cat. "Leave the talking to me."

The cell was small and dimly lit with just a small, metal bed on one side. On the bed sat a young man, perhaps in his twenties or thirties, Arthur guessed. His eyes and face, though, looked much older. Working for the Queen had not been good for him.

"Zane Rackham?" said the Cat.

"Zane Rackham…?" the man repeated in a strange, slightly wavery voice," …yes, he's here. What do you want with him?"

"I want you to tell me about the machine, Rackham," the Cat's voice was low and steady. "I want to know what it's for, where it is and how I can destroy it."

"…the…machine…?" the prisoner looked from the floor to the Cat and back to the floor, "…to control…"

"I think he's still drunk," whispered Teresa.

"Yes, I know the machine is to give the Queen control," the Cat went on. "I want to know about the small part that's about to be completed. Tell me about the small part, Rackham."

"…the names…" the man said again in his strange, unsteady voice, "…give…her…"

Arthur's eyes widened in realisation at what he was seeing. "He isn't drunk," he said. "I think he's gone mad."

The three of them looked and saw it instantly. Zane Rackham had the look of someone who was there and not there all at once. His terrified mind had retreated somewhere far away, hiding itself from… something. Only the bare minimum of Rackham's self was left to control his body.

"Being forced to work for the Queen," the Cat whispered, "to build that terrible machine… he must have seen something that drove him insane."

"Poor man," said Teresa. "I can only imagine what they did to him."

"I don't have to imagine," the Cat said, darkly. "It will have been terrible, I know that. But, unfortunately, we don't have time to play it nice. Let's see if we can shock it out of him."

And with that, the creature suddenly whipped round and leapt right at Rackham, pinning him to the wall with surprising strength and baring teeth which strangely looked ten times larger than they actually were.

"Rackham!" the Cat suddenly shouted at the young man. "I don't have time for this! Tell me about the machine part!"

"...the names... give... her..."

"Tell me!" the Cat shouted again.

"Wait! Listen!" Arthur said, all of a sudden. "He *is* telling you!"

The Cat looked at Arthur, puzzled, then back at the babbling prisoner.

"...the names...give... her... the names... give her... the names...give her... the names..."

"Give her the names..." Arthur said. "Who's 'her'?"

"The Queen, of course," said Teresa before turning to the Cat. "Right?"

But the Cat wasn't speaking right now. He was staring at Zane Rackham.

"It will give her the names?" he said quietly, eventually. "Which names?"

Zane looked deep into the Cat's eyes. "...all of them..."

The Cat looked stunned. The children had no idea why, but it spooked them. Arthur stepped forward.

"Where's the machine part?" he asked.

Zane's manic gaze turned to Arthur, now, and he whispered, "...Waterwhistle."

Now it was Arthur and Teresa's turn to be shocked. Yet it did make such perfect sense, Arthur thought, he wondered why they hadn't guessed it already. It explained why Lady Eris was so busy in the village. Too busy to even chase Arthur in person.

"Where in Waterwhistle is the machine part being built?" Arthur asked. Rackham's gaze became more wild, more disturbed. The man's eyes literally pinned Arthur to the spot.

"Not in a place... no, not in a place," he grabbed Arthur's arm in a vice-like grip. "In the people. It's being built in the *people*..."

Teresa suddenly burst forward, her voice an urgent cocktail of desperation and anger. "How do we destroy it? *Tell me!*"

The prisoner saw Teresa properly for the first time, now. As soon as his eyes locked on her, his eyes and mouth contorted in pure terror.

"No!" he suddenly shouted, scrambling backwards away from Teresa. "Keep away from me! Keep away! Don't let it touch me! *Keep it away from me!!*"

Arthur and the Cat stared at the scene in shock. Zane Rackham, a grown man, was scared to death of Teresa. Not just scared. *Terrified.*

They didn't have any time to figure it out, though. Because that's when the deafening wail of a prison siren blared out from somewhere up the corridor.

"What just happened?" Arthur asked, fearfully.

"We just ran out of time," said the Cat. He turned back to Rackham. The prisoner was cowering away in the corner of the bed, his arms over his eyes.

"Why don't you step away from him, Smithy, my girl?" the Cat said, warily. "Before he has a complete breakdown?"

Teresa nodded in numb confusion and came back to the doorway beside Arthur. The Cat turned back to Rackham.

"I'd bring you with us, Zane," he sounded almost kind, "but you're clearly too unstable. And... I'm really sorry, but they're coming for you. They're going to take you back to the Queen. But somewhere in your head is the key to destroying this monstrous machine you've created. I know you want it destroyed – you wish you'd never been forced to build it. We'll meet again, Zane. And we'll destroy the Agency Engine together. We will. For now, just... just try and stay strong."

Outside, the ominous sound of boots was beginning to echo through the corridors.

"Come on, non-cats."

The Cat led the pair out of the cell. Teresa was the last one out and she turned and looked back at Zane. The dishevelled young man looked back at her. The fear was still there. But something else, too. Something like... pity?

"...in prison too..." was all he said.

"Come on, Smithy!" the Cat shouted and Teresa ran out behind them. The sound of the soldiers was getting closer.

"How are we going to get out?" Arthur said, beginning to fret.

"We could really use one of them famous escapes of yours right now!" Teresa said to the Cat as the sound of tromping boots pounded ever louder.

"Ah, yes, of course," said the Cat. "The third rule of an amazing escape!"

"And what's that..?" Arthur pressed his back against the wall. He noticed the Cat looking above his head and he followed the gaze... straight to a ventilation shaft. A large one.

"Third rule of an amazing escape?" the Cat grinned at Arthur. "Before you do anything, always crank your action music up to full volume!"

THE CHASE

Arthur hung onto the horse's reigns for dear life while the animal galloped as fast as it could go. Teresa, behind, hung onto his waist and the Cat was just behind her, digging his claws into the saddle to keep from tumbling off.

Hot on their heels, seventeen mounted soldiers of the Queen's Guard chased them. Their crimson and black armour shone brightly in the harsh sunlight but the featureless helmets that covered their entire faces dispelled any ideas of dashing knights. They were fearsome, unyielding wraiths and you did *not* want to look behind and see them hot on your tail.

Their swords remained in their scabbards for the time being. However, this was no cause for celebration. The only reason they were not using their swords was because a couple of them were currently bringing long-barrelled rifles to bear.

"I don't want to ever see the inside of a ventilation shaft again!" Teresa shouted over the thundering din of the galloping horses.

"What are you complaining about, Smithy?" the Cat cried back. "We stayed ahead of the guards all the way to the stables, didn't we?"

"We didn't need the stables – we could have used that rat we bumped into in the shaft," Teresa said. "It was big enough to carry the lot of us!"

A gunshot blasted from behind them and shattered a shop window as they flew past.

"We haven't escaped yet!" Arthur yelled, ducking his head.

"Right you are, my lad!" the Cat shouted. "Down there, Arthur! To the left!"

Arthur had no idea what he was doing. He had never ridden a horse before. He'd never run from soldiers trying to kill him before. And he'd never, ever been this terrified before

But he managed to tug hard on the horse's reigns and the animal turned sharply to the left, sprinting down a side road.

"Smithy!" the Cat shouted over the noise of the horse's hooves on the cobbles. "Grab that rifle! The one in the horse's pack near your leg. Give those soldiers something to think about! I'd do it myself but, y'know... paws."

Teresa pulled the long rifle from its holder but then hesitated.

"I... I don't want to shoot anyone..!"

"You're riding on the back of a speeding horse, bobbing all over the place, holding a rifle almost as big as you are, aiming at well trained soldiers on horseback. And you're ten." The Cat grinned at her. "Don't you worry – you're not going to hit *anything*! But it'll make them duck a bit more and shoot at us a bit less. Go on!"

So Teresa hefted the weapon up, rested the butt against her shoulder, aimed it in the general direction of the soldiers.

"Go on!" urged the Cat. "Just pull the tri-"

POW!

"Woah!" Teresa cried. The rifle had kicked backwards in her hands as the bullet blasted out, almost knocking her off the horse. Black smoke from the firearm filled the air for an instant before whipping away as they continued flying forward atop the captured horse.

"Heck of a kick, eh?!" the Cat shouted. It seemed to do the trick, though. The gang of soldiers spread out a little to avoid the incoming shot which meant they were too busy concentrating on not running into each other to bother shooting back.

For the moment, at least.

"Now, this is what I call escaping!" the Cat shouted as the horse took them through another archway and into a rainy part of town.

Far from the excitement in the Cat's voice, Arthur was doing his utmost to control himself. He was so unbelievably terrified, his hands were locked tight around the horse's reigns. He couldn't let go even if he wanted to.

The Cat, on the other hand, sounded like he was playing a game in his back garden. Didn't he realise the seriousness of the situation? Couldn't he tell they were potentially just moments away from death? If he wasn't giving the situation his full attention, then surely Arthur and Teresa were in even *more* danger?

And if all that wasn't enough, they also had absolutely no idea where they were going.

"We're lost!" cried Arthur as they galloped through a green, grassy park. "In case you'd forgotten!"

"Of course we're lost! We're riding around inside a giant, floating maze!" the Cat called. "Don't worry, I have a clever plan!"

"Is your plan to just ride around and hope one of these arches opens up to the docks?" Teresa asked. "Because that's not a plan, that's just laziness."

"Teresa, my dear, you wound me with your lack of faith. Don't you-"

"'Scuse me a sec," Teresa interrupted.

POW!

The soldiers scattered again as Teresa brought the rifle back down.

"Sorry," she said. "You were saying?"

Arthur hung on as the stolen horse took them towards a big archway. They dived through it just before it changed. They were now in a rainy part of the city and the archway behind them switched to show a bustling marketplace.

"We've lost them!" the Cat called out. "They could be anywhere on the island by now."

"So could we," Teresa reminded him, shielding her eyes from the rain. "Wow, you really need to bring an umbrella when you go for a walk in this place – never know *what* kind of weather you'll wander into!"

As they approached the next archway down the road, Arthur was beginning to think about slowing their horse down now they weren't being chased anymore. Problem was, he didn't have the first clue how to do it.

Through the archway ahead of them was a row of houses and what looked like a school. As they approached, the scenery flickered and changed.

And, impossibly, there sat the docks. And the *Galloping Snake*.

"And you thought my laziness wouldn't work!" the Cat grinned at Teresa.

Arthur could have sung with joy! He put his head down and the horse raced towards the arch. They were going to make it! Obviously, Arthur had been worrying about nothi-

The archway changed.

No! Arthur couldn't believe it! Not already!

The docks were gone and they were replaced by...

"Watch out!" shouted the Cat.

The arch had switched to show the road they had just left – the road that still held the Queen's guardsmen. Arthur gaped in shock as he found himself now galloping *towards* the soldiers!

Fortunately, the sudden change had taken the soldiers by surprise too. Before anyone could do anything, both parties found themselves running past each other as they went under the arch. By the time the soldiers were able to react and bring their horses to a halt, they'd run straight past Arthur, Teresa and the Cat – who themselves were now emerging onto the non-rainy side of the archway.

The soldiers, regaining their wits, raised their weapons at their quarry. Unfortunately for them, Teresa's wits were quicker. She was already aiming her rifle at the archway's left supporting strut.

POW!

The wooden column exploded as she hit it dead on. She swiftly aimed at the other strut, on the right.

POW!

Now, both struts were just shreds and the wooden archway creaked and groaned. The soldiers looked up at it, warily, as it swayed to and fro... then with a final sigh, the entire construct crashed to the ground. The rainy street disappeared and the soldiers were gone.

"Nice shootin', Tex!" the Cat bellowed, laughing.

Arthur turned round to see what had happened. That was when everything went very bad.

The horse whinnied in terror as they ran too close to the edge of the road – and the huge openings to the NothingSpace that stretched along there.

The animal reared up in terror as it did its best to avoid falling in. Teresa tumbled off first. Followed by the Cat. And lastly, Arthur. Teresa landed on the ground. The Cat landed on the ground.

Arthur did not.

"Arthur!" Teresa screamed.

"Hang on, Arthur!" shouted the Cat. "Don't let go!"

Arthur's fingers gripped onto the edge of the ground for all they were worth – and the great, gaping NothingSpace yawned out below him.

"Help me!"

"It's okay, Arthur," called the Cat. "Teresa's going to pull you up!"

Even before those words had been spoken, though, Teresa was already on her knees, holding her hand down towards her friend.

"Grab hold!"

Arthur started to reach a hand back up to her -

BANG!

The ground near Arthur's hands exploded in a small puff of smoke and dirt. Teresa fell backwards.

"It's the soldiers!" shouted the Cat. Sure enough, up at the far end of the road, the Queen's men had managed to find their way through another archway and were emerging from it with extreme urgency. Although still some distance away, they were racing up the street toward them, shooting all the time.

Arthur yelled in fear as bullets flew all around him. Little explosions of dirt blew into his face and the **whip** of the bullets whizzing past him seemed to come from all directions at once.

At any moment, he knew he'd be hit. The only way to escape was to let go and fall away into the NothingSpace. But he couldn't do that either. No-one would ever be able to leave the Travel Lines and come looking for him. He'd be alone forever. Alive, and yet, nothing. And at last, he knew why it was a fate worse than death to fall into the NothingSpace.

But it was that or get shot.

Another bit of the ground shattered into a dust cloud right near one of his hands.

"Help me! I'm slipping!" Arthur yelled again. Teresa tried to get to him but loud, cracking gunshots kept forcing her back.

"*NO!*" shouted a deep, powerful, angry voice that Arthur realised with some alarm was coming from the Cat. "Not again!"

And he ran towards the oncoming soldiers. Arthur had no idea what such a tiny cat was going to do to all those massive men in armour but Arthur wasn't really in a position to worry about it.

"Teresa!" he shouted. But there was no answer. Somewhere in the distance, in the direction of the soldiers, Arthur heard an almighty boom, like a crack of thunder. However, he was currently in no frame of mind to wonder what was going on.

Then, all of a sudden, a soldier stepped up to the edge and looked down at Arthur.

This one was dressed differently. Rather than crimson, his armour was a shiny, sky blue. His helmet was different too. Instead of the full-face covering of the

Queen's Guard, this one had a 'T' shape opening through which his eyes, nose and mouth were visible.

It must have been some kind of special soldier, Arthur thought. Sneaked up on them from a different direction while they were busy with the regular ones.

It reached down to him. This was it, Arthur thought, closing his eyes tight. The end. An enormous hand closed around his wrist. What would happen? Would the soldier toss him out into the Black? Or maybe he'd shoot Arthur up close where he couldn't miss.

Arthur felt himself being hoisted into the air with unearthly strength…. and suddenly, the ground was beneath his feet. He opened his eyes.

Teresa was standing next to a second soldier. His armour, helmet and even his face looked identical to the first. But he wasn't holding her and she didn't look captured. The soldier that had lifted Arthur to safety let go of him, gently. Arthur stared numbly from one soldier to the other and over at Teresa. What was going on?

Then Arthur suddenly remembered – the Cat!

He span round to the oncoming Royal Guard… except they were no longer oncoming. They were all lying on the ground. Sprawled and scattered all over the road, their armour ripped open and bits of scarlet metal littered all around. The horses wandered aimlessly around the scene of total devastation. And staggering slowly towards them…

…was the Cat.

"Well, that was quite some exercise…" he panted, "…think I need a lie down now…" and he collapsed.

"Cat!" Teresa ran forward and caught him. Arthur was by her side in an instant.

"Did he really just…" Arthur started, glancing from

the small, furry animal to the bunch of ravaged guardsmen, "…I mean…*all* those soldiers..?"

"I don't know," Teresa said. "I wasn't watching, I was trying to get to you. Then these two other soldiers turned up…"

A distant rattling noise interrupted Teresa. The group looked up to see another mounted squad of Guardsmen coming charging out of the archway at the end of the road. Swords were drawn and rifles were ready as they powered towards the unconscious Cat and his allies.

"Bamboo sent us," one of the blue soldiers suddenly said in a deep voice which Arthur thought sounded vaguely Russian. "He is thinking you might be needing our help. Looks like he is thinking right."

The soldier who had rescued Arthur held out a piece of paper to the young boy.

"Is map. Follow it back to ship," he said.

Arthur took it, warily.

"And we are not soldiers," he said as they both turned to the oncoming attackers and drew their swords. "We are knights."

And they ran into the oncoming soldiers.

Arthur and Teresa watched, mouths open in awe as the two blue knights ploughed into the Queen's guard. They swung their huge swords left and right and scarlet-clad soldiers went flying in all directions, screaming. It was like watching a monstrous ocean wave crashing down onto the shore, blasting away everything before it.

"Come on!" Teresa called to Arthur while cradling the Cat's unmoving body as carefully as possible. "We need to get going!"

Tearing his gaze away from the destruction unfolding

before him, Arthur scrambled to his feet and, following the knights' map, led Teresa through the streets.

The paper gave Arthur all the instructions he needed. They ran up and down various roads and waited at the archways for the right amount of time in order for them to switch to the correct destination. And all the while, the only thing going through Arthur's mind was the blackness below his feet as he dangled from the edge of the world...

"Here we are!" Teresa shouted. And sure enough, Arthur had led them right back to the docks. And there *finally* was the *Galloping Snake* waiting for them.

"Wondered where you lot had gotten yerselves to," Captain Thrace leaned casually on the railings. "Stopped for a spot o' lunch with the Governor, did ye?"

That's when he saw the Cat's unconscious body and stood up straight, suddenly aware of the seriousness of the situation.

BOOM!

An explosion rocked the docks and the trio looked up to see the two blue knights came running round the corner at full speed. Even clad in full body, metal armour, they moved extremely fast. Thrace immediately drew his weapon and took aim at them.

"Damn kids, ye've got 'em right on yer tail!"

"No!" Teresa shouted.

Arthur pulled the gun down before Thrace could take a shot. "They're with us!"

Thrace eyed the pair of knights suspiciously as they ran up the gangplank and joined them.

"My name is Iakob," said one knight before pointing to the other. "And this is my brother Iosef."

"Yakob and Yosef, eh?" Thrace tried his best to

pronounce the unusual names. "So... ye *haven't* got 'em right on yer tail...?"

That's when fifty horse-mounted soldiers came charging round the corner.

"No, you were right first time," said Iakob. "They are definitely on tail!"

The Captain wasted no more time and raced over to the ship's wheel.

"Pull up the gangplank! Release the clamps!" he shouted. "An' raise the sails!"

Arthur didn't move – he couldn't take his eyes off the advancing soldiers. Every muscle in his body had frozen stiff with fear. Teresa handed him the Cat and ran to help the Captain get the ship in flight.

Arthur watched as Iakob and Iosef ran back down the gangplank and started fighting off the soldiers to slow them down and buy the *Snake* enough time to get going. He watched as the ship finally began to move off, up away from the quayside. And he watched as the knights both launched into unbelievably massive leaps and landed on the deck just as Captain Thrace threw the lever all the way forward, filling the sails with the impossible wind.

And soon, Arthur was watching Labyrinth as it floated away into the dark and was gone. He heard Teresa and Thrace whooping with joy and Iakob and Iosef clasp each other's hands. But he looked down and saw the unconscious body of the Cat in his arms.

Didn't anyone else get it? Didn't they understand?

The Cat was always in control. He always knew what to do and he always found it exciting. But this time, the Cat was lying in Arthur's arms, out cold. He wasn't in control anymore.

And Arthur finally realised the answer he should have given when Bamboo had asked if he wanted to leave.

I told you that you'd regret it, didn't I?

THE HORSE AND HER MAN
(from the somewhat self-absorbed thoughts of Mary the Horse)

It's getting late into the evening as I trot through the centre of the village. We've had a busy couple of days ferrying things to and fro. Fruit. Veg. People to see Bamboo. And do I get a word of thanks from that annoying man sitting back there atop my cart?

"Well?" I ask him. "Do I?"

Elian sighs. "How many times do I have to tell you, horse, there's no point in having most of the conversation in your head and only bringing me in right at the end. I have no idea what you're going on about! Do you *what?*"

"Get any thanks? From you!"

"Thanks for what? For walking?"

"Takes more effort than sitting. Just saying."

"Who do you think lines up all our work?" he asks me. "People don't just come along and drop it in our lap, you know. I have to go out and bring the jobs in. You're lucky to have someone as experienced as me running things."

"By 'experienced', do you mean 'old'?" I snigger. "And by 'running things', do you mean 'sitting on your backside while your poor horse does all the *real* work'?"

"If I'm old, it's because you make me old with your constant nagging."

"I don't nag – I just tell you when you go wrong. Is it my fault you go wrong a lot?"

"Do you know what Bamboo told me once? That in the human world, an old horse is sometimes called a Nag."

Elian laughed long and loud. "Now if that's not the most appropriate name I ever heard…!"

"Oh, buzz off!" I neigh.

"Buzz *this*," and I hear and feel the sharp **crack** of Elian's riding whip on my rump.

"Ouch!" I can't believe it! "Right, that's it!"

I stop walking – right there in the middle of the road. Some of the other carts and pedestrians shout at me as they go past. I don't care.

"I'm not going anywhere until I get an apology from you, Elian Mahaan. We've had this conversation before! No whips!"

Hah! See how he likes it now! I'll show him who's in charge. I'll show him what-

Eh?

I can feel the cart shake in that telltale way that lets me know that Elian's jumped off. He walks in front of me, stretching his arms out in front of him.

"Right you are, then, Mary," he says, putting his hands to the small of his back and stretching that too. "You stand there for as long as you like. I'm going to get a beer."

That's when I realise I stopped in front of a pub.

Drat. I could have planned *that* better.

I turn to see Elian strolling towards the tavern, no doubt already tasting that foul ale that those odd, two-leggers like so much.

But then, all of a sudden, three men in black suits appear out of nowhere and approach him. One of them is carrying a little black, bag. They're all a little too far away for me to hear what they're saying over the din of the street.

Then – oh, my stars! – the men are bundling Elian away from the tavern door and down the alley by the side of the building.

Frantically, I look around for help but no-one else seems to have noticed anything. I turn back and am about to call out his name...

...when, all of a sudden, he comes strolling back out of the alleyway all by himself. As if nothing ever happened. Instead of going into the tavern, he comes back over to me.

"Are... are you okay?" I ask. "What was that all about?"

"Oh, just a couple of robbers, wanting my money," Elian says. "I soon saw them off. School boxing champion, eight years in a row at school, didn't I ever tell you?"

I roll my eyes. "You might have mentioned it once or twice..."

Then, I look down the now empty alleyway.

"They were dressed awfully nicely for robbers," I say, doubtfully.

"Yes, Mary, that's because they'd already stolen those clothes from someone else," Elian laughs. "It's what robbers do, you silly horse. I'm... very sorry about using my whip before, by the way. I know you don't like it. I promise not to do it again." He flicks my reigns, lightly. "Come on, then, let's get on."

"I thought you were going for a beer," I say to him, suspicious of his sudden change in mood. "I thought you needed a break from my constant nagging."

"Oh, no," he grins (a strange, new grin, I think). "I like to hear you talk. Why else would I sit here day after day all these years? Come on, tell me everything. I'm a good listener. For instance, I never asked you if you overheard

- 197 -

any gossip when the Cat and his friends were here before."

"Ah, well," I whinnie as we start to trot along again. "I think my old ears did pick up a little slice or two..."

And we wander along. It's nice for Elian to finally be listening to me for a change.

THE NAME GAME

The Captain's cabin was awash with noise.

Sitting around the large, square, wooden table was Teresa, the Cat, Iakob, Iosef and Captain Thrace himself. Every single one of them was talking at the same time. The only person at the table not saying a word was Arthur.

When the Cat had regained consciousness, everyone had wanted to know how he'd defeated that entire squad of soldiers all by himself. He'd made some kind of joke and deftly avoided talking about it. But it was clear to Arthur the Cat was hiding something. Some important, serious piece of information that he was covering up with a joke. But, then, Arthur thought, wasn't that just like the Cat? Just like the whole 'used to be a King' thing. The Cat only said what he wanted people to know and he hid the rest.

Arthur's eyes were fixed firmly on the rough, pock-marked wooden table-top in front of him. Somewhere around the edge of his hearing was the nonsensical babbling on about names and machines – but all he could really hear were the non-stop cracks of the peacekeeper weapons. All he could really see was the endless Black reaching up for him…

"Okay, will anyone who is not a Cat please, *SHUT UP!*" the Cat's voice suddenly cut though the pea-soup fog around Arthur's brain as well as the babble of noise in the room. Everyone instantly fell silent and stared at the small, black feline.

"*Thank* you…" he sighed. "Gosh, it's like school on the last day of term! Now, Smithy…" he turned to Teresa.

"…since you asked about the significance of the Queen stealing names, I'll explain."

Arthur's mind was back in the present for the moment so he tried to focus his attention on the meeting. He wondered if all this talk of names had anything to do with what the Cat told him on the night they met – about the way Lady Eris made Arthur feel weak and scared every time she said his name.

"Your name," began the Cat, "is the most important thing about you. It makes you who you are. It carries your core energy. And if someone knows your name, they can control that core energy. They can control *you*."

Teresa wrinkled her nose in disbelief. "Really…?"

"Oh, it's not just an Arilon thing," the Cat went on. "Many cultures in the Human World know this, too. Your all-powerful, scientific, modern-minded people might think this is nonsense but even they know how to manipulate people by the use of their names. They do it all the time.

"Think about it. When you're a bit bored at school and you can't be bothered to listen to the teacher…"

"I'm sure I don't know what you mean!" Teresa winked at Arthur. "I *always* pay attention in school!"

Arthur felt himself smile back at her a little, despite his mood.

"*Teresa Frances Smith!*" the Cat shouted.

Immediately, Teresa stopped smiling, sat up straight and gave the Cat her full attention.

"Sorry," she said.

The Cat smiled. "You see? That worked a lot better than me simply saying 'stop messing about'. Because I used your name. I said it in a certain way. You didn't realise it, but I manipulated your core energy. I controlled you. Just a

- 200 -

little. I made you do what I wanted, which was to stop talking."

Teresa was awestruck. "Wow... you're right! My father's always doing that! Bet he didn't realise he was being a sorcerer..!"

"Now imagine such power in hands of Queen," said Iakob in that strong, Russian-sounding accent. "Imagine Queen with names of all Arilon people in palm of her hand."

"She'd be able to control everyone," Arthur said, nodding. "Completely. No more cutting Travel Lines. No more messing about."

"But..." Teresa said, suddenly, "couldn't people hide their names? Like you, Cat, and the Queen."

"It's not so easy to do," said the Cat. "To a Weaver, your name is kind of like those shops with the huge, signs on the front made out of light-bulbs. It's very, very visible. It takes great skill and cunning to hide it. Being totally brilliant, I – of course – have such skill and cunning. Unfortunately, so does the Queen. Very few other people do."

"So, that is it..." said Iosef. "When Queen completes part of machine in Waterwhistle, she wins. She has control over everyone in Arilon."

The Cat nodded. "Nobody will be able to stop her from completing the rest of the Agency Engine."

"But..." Teresa said, a dark realisation heavy in her voice, "...having control over everyone in Arilon... that's already a huge thing, isn't it? I mean... if just this little part of the Agency Engine allows her to do *that*... what would the *full* power of the machine do..?"

The room was silent, now, as the full force of that question hit home with everyone around the table.

"That…" said the Cat, finally, "…is a question we don't want answered the hard way."

Teresa gulped.

"Still…" the Cat shrugged. "It's better to know what you're dealing with rather than sticking your head in the -"

"I want to go home."

Those five words, so softly spoken, stopped everyone in their tracks. They turned to the person that had said them.

They turned to Arthur.

"…what…?" the disbelief in Teresa's voice cut into Arthur's chest as surely as a knife. But it didn't deter him.

"I want to home," he said again. "I thought I'd be able to help you all. But, after Labyrinth… and now this… I'd just get in the way. I'll end up getting one of you hurt or killed if I stay. It's best if I just…"

That's right, scaredy-cat.
Tell them it's because you're worried about them.
Don't tell them the truth. Don't tell them you're just so scared,
you want to run home and bury your head
in your pillow and hope it all goes away…

Iakob and Iosef watched Arthur, their faces, undersanding. They didn't know the boy well but they could see he was not cut out for this kind of adventure. It was best for him that he go home and leave this to the others.

Captain Thrace's mouth was cocked ever-so-slightly up at one end and it reminded Arthur of one thing. Lady

- 202 -

Eris' smile when she saw how right she'd been that Arthur was a coward.

The Cat watched Arthur with a completely unreadable expression. Arthur couldn't decide if it was understanding or disappointment. Acceptance or disgust.

The worst face, though, the one that pained him the most to see... was Teresa's. She was angry and aghast, yes. But under it all, she was hurt.

"I'm sorry..." Arthur said to everyone (but he was looking at Teresa when he said it), "...I'm just... I'm sorry..."

Teresa's chair scraped heavily backwards, cutting through the silence as sure as a bell and she ran quickly from the room, slamming the door behind her.

The Cat finally spoke.

"Captain Thrace," he said quietly. "Please set course for Graft."

HOMEWARD

It had seemed to Arthur that they'd reached Graft in no time at all.

He'd spent the entire jouney sitting below in Captain Thrace's cabin while everyone else went about their business elsewhere on the ship.

Finally, they'd arrived and the Cat brought Arthur up on deck. Iakob, Iosef and Captain Thrace all shook Arthur's hand and wished him luck. (There was a strange look on the old Captain's face, Arthur thought – as though he couldn't quite decide if he was glad Arthur was getting off his ship or not).

Teresa, unfortunately, didn't shake Arthur's hand. And she didn't wish him good luck. In fact, she didn't even make an appearance.

"She's upset..." Captain Thrace said, uncertainly, clearly unpracticed in the matters of crew emotional problems, "...but I'm sure she'll miss ye, just the same..."

Arthur had just nodded and the Cat had led him down the gangplank and into the silent docks. It was the middle of the night on Graft and there was absolutely no-one around. It was very odd to see the place so quiet considering how busy it had been before. He supposed, though, that if people on the island worked so hard all the time, sleep was something they took very seriously indeed.

Thinking about this, he realised he was going to miss Arilon very much. But his decision was the right one. He absolutely had to-

Run away.

The Cat led Arthur in a new direction, away from the Broken Crown. They headed out of the main part of the town and into an area that Arthur quickly realised was full of vegetable allotments. The small plots of green and brown, splashed with the muted night-time colour of the gas lamps all reminded Arthur of his uncle's little vegetable patch. It was strange how even though they were in another world, some things were exactly the same as back home.

Arthur forced himself to push such thoughts from his mind. At first, Arilon had been a totally alien place but more and more, it was feeling familiar and normal. As though it wasn't really another world, just an extension of the one he knew. Like another country or something.

And he didn't like to think of the Queen destroying it.

Before long, they had arrived at a small shed with a wooden rack outside it upon which hung a range of rusty, worn out tools.

In front of the ramshackle, old building, at the foot of the doorway, was a small mat. It was worn and brown, clearly having had the owner's muddy boots scraped across its surface for years. And yet, the picture of a row of carrots that was woven into it was still just about visible – as though the mat simply refused to let it go.

The Cat moved his paw over the mat, copying the symbols on the paper Bamboo had given him.

Then he turned to Arthur.

"That's it," he said, finally. "Step on. It'll take you home."

Arthur stared at the mat. "That's it? No sparkles, no... flashing lights?"

"Portal magic is difficult but pretty unspectacular," said the Cat. "The mat is now a gateway. Once you're through, I'll turn it back into a mat."

"And this will take me back to London?"

The Cat nodded.

Arthur took a deep breath and looked at it. "Okay..."

"Flying the *Galloping Snake*, single-handedly," the Cat said, suddenly. Arthur looked up.

"Excuse me?"

"Your favourite bit. Am I right?"

A small smile crept onto Arthur's face. "It was pretty amazing..." But then the smile faded as his mind turned back to Labyrinth.

"You did very well, Arthur Arthur Ness," said the Cat.

Arthur looked into the Cat's eyes. Once, at school, Arthur had run the hundred yards dash in P.E. He'd come last by such a large margin that the other children were already back sitting down when he'd crossed the finish line. The teacher had told him he'd 'done very well'. But the look in the teacher's eyes told Arthur that the teacher didn't mean it.

It was the same look Arthur saw in the Cat's eyes now.

All of a sudden, an anger rose in Arthur's chest. He'd had enough of Arilon. Enough of the Cat. Enough of the Queen, of Lady Eris. Enough of everything.

He stepped forward onto the mat.
And he was home.
In London.
In the hallway of his own house.

BLITZED

"Mum?"

Arthur shouted at the top of his voice. He was back in his hallway, standing on the old, raggedy mat his dad had brought back from Burma. Arthur had never really liked it but right now it was the best raggedy old mat in the world.

"Mum?!" Arthur shouted again.

That's when he noticed the place was an absolute wreck.

Dark, violent, cracks jagged their way up the walls, furniture was smashed and scattered all over the floor, windows were broken. What was going on?

"Mum, where are you?"

Still, no answer. Through the front door's glass panelling, Arthur could see it was night. But a much darker night than you could ever normally expect in the city. It was the Blackout.

An air raid was in progress.

To make it harder for the enemy bombers to find their targets, all houses had to turn their lights off and put thick curtains on the windows to hide the candle-light. Arthur had even helped his mum put black tape on the windows to keep them from shattering too badly if they got smashed by a nearby explosion.

In Arilon, Arthur thought, the Black was to be avoided at all costs. Here, in London, it kept you safe.

Everything was as he expected it to be during a Blackout with only his mother in the house.

Everything except... no mother.

Arthur went from room to room in the dark. Living room. Front room. Kitchen. All just a crumbling half-wrecked mess. Surely she wouldn't have stayed here alone, Arthur thought? Maybe she was at Mrs. Patterson's down the road? Unless Mrs. Patterson's wasn't there any more. This kind of damage to the house... surely that meant somewhere nearby had been totally flattened.

Arthur went slowly upstairs. The creaking of the steps was the only sound in the cold, dark, silent house. His parents' room was as much of a mess as everywhere else. He went to his own bedroom.

To Arthur's astonishment, it was in perfect condition! Not so much as a book out of place.

Not knowing what else to do, Arthur sat on the end of his bed and looked up at the ceiling – at the mobile he and his father had made. Two spitfires circling round each other, keeping Arthur safe as he slept. He remembered sitting right on that spot, looking up at those planes on the morning he left, just as his mother had come into the room.

"You have to be brave," she said, sitting down next to Arthur. His suitcase was sitting patiently by the side of the bed. His coat-label with the Waterwhistle address rested ontop of it. Waiting for him.

"Brave like dad?" Arthur asked.

"Brave like *all* those pilots."

"But... aren't they scared?"

And Arthur's mother had smiled. "Of course they are."

Arthur was puzzled and was about to ask her how they could be brave and scared at the same time – when an insistent **honk honk** intruded from the street below.

"Come on," said his mother, picking up the suitcase and that horrid, hated label. "The bus is here. We need to get to the station, or we're going to miss your train."

Arthur couldn't take his eyes off the paper fighter planes now, as they hung motionless above him. He knew his dad was flying one of them right now, somewhere many miles away. He could almost hear the humming of their engines.

Wait... he *could* hear plane engines. And they were getting louder. But how could-

BOOM!

The entire world shook and the light of a thousand suns came pouring in through the bedroom window. Time suddenly seemed to slow down, come almost to a complete halt... Arthur could almost see the individual cracks moving slowly along the glass, spidering outwards, joining up with each other... time crawled almost to a halt, until time became *now* and all of a sudden everything's happening *right this moment* with powerful clarity and terror.

And time cranks back up to full speed – and the window explodes, sending glass flying everywhere. Arthur lies on the floor, surrounded by bits of razor-sharp window... the tape not having done such a great job on this occasion. But Arthur knows that means the explosion had been very close.

The bright light has faded back to night-time again but with a faint, orange after-glow. Arthur looks out of the window. Fire. Several streets away. The high street. Maybe closer.

In bomb terms, a very near miss.

But then, more humming. More planes. Arthur runs. He gets as far as the stairs.

BOOM!

This one – even closer – and the whole house seems to jump clear off the ground with the shock of the nearby impact as Arthur is thrown down the stairs, head over heels. Huge chunks of ceiling and wall and floor are leaping and falling in every direction.

Arthur knows he's completely unprotected. He has to get out. He runs to the front door and turns the latch, pulling it.

It won't open! Stupid, stupid – this time of night, surely it's been locked. Plus, the shaking of the house has probably shifted it in its frame so it's totally jammed in place. What to do now?

In a flash, it comes to Arthur. Back door!

He turns, runs down the hallway towards the kitchen and the back door but-

CRASH

The entire ceiling suddenly drops down in front of him – Arthur glimpses bits of his parents' bedroom furniture – their bed, their wardrobes – falling into the kitchen before the entire doorway is filled with rubble.

Arthur's mind goes numb and his heart starts to beat even faster. He's trapped! Can't go forward, can't go back. He runs back to the middle of the hallway. No idea what to do, where to go. He looks up. The front door has indeed shifted in its frame – it's dropped down several inches and there's a gap between the top of the door and the doorframe. And through it, Arthur can see the night sky. He can see the glow of fire and draping of thick smoke.

And he can see a plane. An enemy bomber.

Flying straight towards him.

And a dot…

…coming out of the bottom of the plane.

Oh, no.

A bomb.

Coming straight towards his house. Straight towards *him*.

Nowhere he can go. Nothing he can do.

It gets closer. Arthur can almost see the design, the writing on the side of the bomb.

It'll hit in just a second.

Wait, what's that? Something tugging..? Arthur looks down.

He's standing on the raggedy, old rug.

There's something poking out of the rug, grabbing Arthur's shoelace.

A cat's paw.

It pulls hard.

Arthur falls into the rug.

NEEDLED

And Arthur was back. Back in Arilon. Back in the nighttime garden in front of the ramshackle shed, standing on the threadbare, muddy mat that-

"*RUN!*" the Cat shouted with such volume and urgency, Arthur almost fell over.

"But...what..." Arthur stammered. The Cat grabbed his shoelaces and tugged with an amazing, paranormal strength.

"Arthur, run *now!*" the Cat shouted again. "It's the *Needlemen!*"

Arthur's mind was a whirl of questions – Needlemen? What are Needlemen? Why are they here? Why is the Cat *afraid*...

All of which were immediately cut off as Arthur staggered backwards and tripped over the body of Frogham, lying on the ground.

The whirl in Arthur's mind only got faster and more confusing. Nothing was making any sense. So he did the only thing he could think to do when nothing made any sense.

He trusted the Cat.

He got up and his ran for his life.

The pair of them sprinted through the allotments, through cabbages and potatoes and carrots, running from what, Arthur didn't know. All he knew was that he was terrified.

"You took me by surprise, Cat!" Frogham's voice rang out from behind them. "You knocked me down before I could grab yer! You won't get another chance!"

"You shan't escape, feline! Not this time!" Another voice, well-spoken, one that Arthur didn't recognise. But that voice wasn't behind them. It was off to their left.

Arthur looked round as he ran, trying to spot the owner of the new voice. All he could see were sheds and greenhouses and bushes and spades and vegetables all appearing out of the dark ahead of them and disappearing into the dark behind them. The dark that hid their pursuers.

Suddenly-

Thwip!

– a shiny, gossamer-thin wire shot out of the darkness from one side, right across the front of the escaping pair and stuck into a shed on the other side. The Cat narrowly darted out of the way and Arthur barely managed to skid to a halt before he hit it. He could see, even in the dark, as light from the nighttime sun glinted off the wire that it was razor-sharp. If he'd run into it, it might have cut him in half!

Another voice, this time from the other side.

"You're ours now, Cat, you and the boy!"

That one, Arthur *did* recognise – the old man with the talking horse from Bamboo's island. What was *he* doing here on Graft? What were all these people doing, chasing them?!

"Come on!" the Cat shouted and he started to shoot off in another direction – but another glistening wire whipped out of the darkness and embedded itself into a tree right next to Arthur.

The pair turned around to yet another direction but another wire *thwipped* by, cutting them off once again. Then another. And another. And another. From all directions. Hemming them in, closing them off. And before long, there was a massive web of wires stretching off in all directions, glistening, deadly-sharp, in the pale lamplight.

Arthur knew the Cat could still have escaped – he was small, fast and agile – but he went nowhere.

He stayed by Arthur's side.

As they both stood there, trapped, figures began to emerge from the misty darkness. Frogham. An old man in a neat suit that Arthur didn't recognise. And finally, Elian from Bamboo's island, just as Arthur had guessed.

But that wasn't all.

Appearing out of the night were another three or four men in dark suits and wide-brimmed hats. Long shadows were cast down their faces and only their mouths could be seen protruding from the darkness beneath the hat-brims. But even seeing only the mouths was enough because the thin lips on each and every mouth was twisted up in a horrible, horrible smile. The same smiles that Frogham and the other two were wearing.

And so, at last, Arthur's unasked questions were answered.

These were Needlemen.

They were here to capture them.

And the Cat was afraid of them because they could become and replace anyone. Including his closest friends.

"Told yer it was pointless to run," said the fake Frogham. "Time ter come with us."

Raising a massive, meaty hand, fake Frogham pulled delicately on one of the wires and they all immediately flew towards Arthur and the Cat in a storm of lethal, flashing light until Arthur's arms and hands were fastened tight to his body and his feet were bound together with just enough slack to allow him to walk. Looking back at the Cat, Arthur could see a wire had wrapped itself around the Cat's neck and connected him to Arthur, forcing the feline to walk slowly behind.

Panic began to lick at the edges of Arthur's mind and he started to pull and thrash at his bonds.

"Arthur, no!" the Cat cried. "The wires will just tighten the more you struggle! You'll end up cutting your arms off!"

Arthur cried out as the wires began to dig into his wrists, drawing a thin, sharp line of blood. He decided to take the Cat's advice and forced himself to calm down.

Quickly, the Needlemen marched Arthur and the Cat away from the allotments, through the town and back to the docks. As they were about to turn the last corner before the part of the docks where the *Galloping Snake* was moored, the Cat spoke.

"Arthur, I'm very sorry, but you're going to have to be very brave at what comes next. It won't be easy. In fact, it'll be very, very hard. The hardest thing that you've ever had to do. Please just remember who you really are. And remember what you really want."

Arthur wanted to turn his head and look at the Cat. What did he mean? What was he talking about? Remember who he was, what he wanted? But he never got the chance because they turned a corner and entered the docks. And Arthur's body flooded with terror at what he saw.

A ship – collosal in size – was moored next to the *Snake*. It dwarfed Captain Thrace's ship by at least three times and was built entirely of a deep, black wood. Several ropes and cables snaked from the looming, malevolent ship and were hooked into the hull of the *Snake*, holding it firmly in place and keeping it from escaping.

The huge letters on the other ship's nameplate confirmed for Arthur just what he'd expected.

The ship was called *The Noir*.

The Needlemen marched the pair up the gangplank of the massive, imperious-looking galleon and onto her deck. As expected, Iakob, Iosef and Teresa were tied up and held captive by Yarnbulls. As expected, Lady Eris was standing there, staring at Arthur and the Cat, triumph gleaming in her eyes.

What was *not* expected was that Captain Thrace was standing by her side.

"Traitor!" the Cat hissed at the old pirate.

"Oh, don't be like that," Lady Eris said, smoothly. "Captain Thrace might have betrayed your location to me but my Needlemen were on your trail anyway. They had almost caught up with you. Captain Thrace simply made the inevitable happen today instead of tomorrow."

"It's nothin' personal, Cat," said the Captain. "I could see you lot weren't no match for Lady Eris, here. I just didn't want to be on the losin' side. But you *were* right, about one thing," the Captain held up a handful of gold coins. "She *is* rich!"

Arthur glanced around the deck. It was like a bigger, darker, more dangerous version of the *Galloping Snake*. And where Arthur was used to seeing Captain Thrace's ship all but deserted, this one was filled with crew, soldiers and a smattering of Yarnbulls.

"Like it, Arthur?" grinned the Cat as though he was having a conversation over a bowl of fizzy milk at the Broken Crown. "Big ship, isn't it? It's called the *Noir*. Used to be called the *Aerie*. Then they had to change it to the *Kray*. After that, the *Taranteen*. Every time I defeated one of the Noir Ladies, they had to change its name for its new owner. In the end, I got rid of so many of them, they just gave up, didn't they, Eris? Re-named it the *Noir* and had done with it."

The Cat turned his attention fully to Lady Eris now, his voice not as light. Not as friendly. "The Queen's got her head screwed on straight, hasn't she, Eris? She knows how many of her Noir Ladies I've done away with. Just like I'm going to do away with you. Because no matter how many of you creatures she throws at me, I just keep coming. And before you know it, you'll be stitched into the walls of your mistress's chamber along with your predecessors."

The triumphant grin faded from Lady Eris' face and was replaced with something that Arthur had seen back when the Cat had revealed himself to her, right before they'd escaped through the tapestry. She was afraid of him.

The Cat smiled at Lady Eris now, but it had no humour or warmth or friendliness in it at all. It had teeth and terror and it made Arthur feel as though he didn't really know the Cat at all. And that somehow, the way he looked – small and black and slim – was not at all the whole story.

"You know you can't win, Eris. You're evil, your mistress is evil and ontop of that... you've hurt my friends," he growled. "All of which means I will defeat you. You know it's coming. And then it's only a matter of time before the Queen finds herself under my claws once again. And this time, I won't hesitate to finish the job."

Emboldened by her position, Lady Eris r fear away and her mocking sneer returned.

"No more escaping, Cat. No more running. And no more Noir Ladies falling before you. Not ever again. The story ends here." Lady Eris smiled and turned to Arthur. "Is that not right, Arthur Ness?"

She pointed at Arthur and black threads flooded out of the end of her finger and shot straight toward Arthur's head and face and eyes... and the last thing he heard before darkness claimed him was Teresa screaming his name.

THE END OF THE NIGHTMARE
(from the no-longer-scared thoughts of Arthur Ness)

My eyes snap open.

I take a deep breath. And another. Slowly, calm comes over me and I realise where I am.

My bedroom!

Perfectly tidy and not blown to bits. And the morning sunshine pouring through the not-smashed window.

"Arthur?" The door opens and in walks... no... it *can't* be...

"I heard a noise, are you okay?"

With a sudden surge of energy, I leap out of bed and give my mother the hugest, tightest hug I've ever given her.

"Wow, what did I do to deserve this?" she laughs, hugging me back. "I haven't had one of these for a long time!"

"I'm just so glad to see you," I mumble into her shoulder. "I've had the most terrible nightmare."

From somewhere deep inside me, there's a voice shouting, telling me that something's wrong. And I think I can hear a woman's evil laugh. But I silence it all and shut it away. There's nothing wrong.

I'm exactly where I wanted to be all along.

"Well, don't worry. It's over," she whispers back to me. "It wasn't real. You're awake now."

TO BE
CONCLUDED

The Chronicles of Arilon continue…

ARTHUR NESS
and the
SECRET OF WATERWHISTLE

PART 2

The magical land of Arilon and the human village of Waterwhistle are trembling in fear. The evil Lady Eris and her shadowy mistress, the Queen stand ready to activate the Agency Engine and take control of every man, woman and child in both places.

Arthur and Teresa, two children from Waterwhistle, find themselves embroiled in the battle to stop activation of the Engine at all costs. To do that, they need to find a way to free the trapped warriors of the bravery island, Valia. They have to locate the ultimate weapon by enlisting the aid of the elusive Blind Dressmaker. And they have to find a way past the massed forces of the Queen's Royal Fleet and get back home to help their family and friends still entranced by Lady Eris' web of fear.

Before any of that, though, Teresa has to find a way out of Lady Eris' dungeons along with her friends, the mysterious Cat and the twin knights, Iakob and   Iosef. And Arthur? Arthur is trapped in a devious prison from which no-one has ever escaped.

If Arthur and Teresa are to discover the secret of Waterwhistle and defeat Lady Eris, one thing's for sure – they have a lot of work to do.

JOIN THE CAT ONLINE

Enjoyed spending time in Arilon? Well, there's no need to leave! Head over to The Arilon Chronicles website to find out more about the islands or get clues on what's coming up next. You can even leave a comment on what you think of the story so far. Just don't forget to bring some fish for the Cat...

www.arilon-chronicles.com

40588889R00139

Printed in Poland
by Amazon Fulfillment
Poland Sp. z o.o., Wrocław